REDEEM ME

THE LAST VOCARI
BOOK THREE

ELENA LAWSON

THORN HOUSE
PUBLISHING

CHAPTER 1

*I*n my state of unconsciousness, I dreamed feverishly of all the ways I wanted to punish Azrael for his stupid mistake. How could he have let Raphael get away?

We *had* him.

On the brink of consciousness, I skimmed through a few more options, painting them in vivid—if a little morbid—pictures in my mind. *I could pull off his finger-nails. Oh, I know! How about chop off all that pretty hair? Oh! Oh! Or I could just fucking lob his stupid handsome head off with my katana and be done with it.*

Except, I wouldn't ever be able to do any of those things. Azrael was the oldest vampire to ever live, along-side his twin brother. I might as well have been a mouse facing down a fucking lion.

But he would be made to feel the heat of my fury one way or another, just as soon as I could peel back my goddamned eyelids and *wake up*. My mind floated up once more from the pit of my unconsciousness, as it had been doing for a couple of days now, but this time, I gripped tight to the thread pulling me awake, resolved not to let it escape.

I moaned painfully, but barely any sound escaped my lips, stopped by the raw dryness in my throat. A stab of something like a hot knife pressed into the top of my skull. *Ouch.*

A pinch in my right hand when I tried to move told me there was an IV jabbed into my vein there. And the chill of fluids being pumped inside told me that Azrael seemed to be *giving* me fluids this time. Not taking them from me as he usually did.

That's new.

A tight breath drawn in through chapped lips almost made me choke. I thought I was back inside the cave with Azrael, but now I wasn't so sure.

The air wasn't stale and fetid like it was down there. It was crisp and scented lightly of lavender. And if the light I could see staining the front of my eyelids in a white glow didn't lie, then I was in a room with normal lighting, not the flickering orange glow of torchlight.

I could've kissed Azrael for not dumping me back down in that awful pit he called a home, but it didn't excuse his idiocy. I'd thank him…after I hit him a good few times.

My lips parted and an awful hissing croak fell from them instead of the words I'd meant to say.

A shuffling of feet over soft carpet. The scents of worn leather and tangy aftershave filled my nose. *Frost.*

"Water," I tried again, slitting my eyes open for half a second before squeezing them shut again against the searing brightness.

His hand brushed something from my face, and I felt the last bits of my consciousness emerging from sleep. "What?" he crooned, and I could picture the worried crease in his brow. See the tense lines of his chiseled face, even with my eyes shut.

"Fucking *water*," I repeated, and the words came out more clearly. "Please," I added as an afterthought.

Frost's large arm slid under my back and I winced as his hand passed over a particularly tender spot just between my shoulder blades. He lifted me to sitting and my body sagged. My head almost lolled back before I managed to engage the muscles in my neck.

I blinked my eyes open, gritting my teeth as they adjusted to the bright lights. Cool glass touched my lips, and I lifted my hands shakily to tip the contents down my parched throat.

"More?" Frost asked.

I nodded, and he propped me up, as though I weighed no more than a doll, against a mountain of pillows and slid his arm out from under me.

He returned with a second glass, and this time I didn't need his help to hold it to my lips. I took it from him with hands that were already steadying and greedily gulped it down. I shivered as the cool liquid snaked down my esophagus and pooled in my stomach.

"Better?"

"Mmm," I replied and handed him the empty glass,

tipping my head to audibly crack my neck, working out the kinks. My eyes regained their focus, and I realized I had absolutely no idea where we were.

The room was grandiose. The bedframe was filigreed gold with a tall headboard and four poster columns on each corner, spiraling up almost to the ceiling. The sheets were satiny smooth off-white Egyptian cotton. The carpet was plush, velvety plum, and the crown-molding was something you might find in a French chateau, or maybe a castle. Except the enormous window, draped in heavy gold tasseled curtains across from me was entirely sealed off by a black metal shutter drawn down over it.

It looked so out of place among all the antique finery that I did a double take.

It all came back to me in a rush of memories I'd rather have stayed forgotten. In my fevered dreams, my mind had fixated on Azrael. And on Raphael...and how the bastard was somehow still breathing, that I'd forgotten all about the other horrors.

The guys. *My* guys. Their home was destroyed. Ethan's shop reduced to a burning orange inferno. Everything they worked for. Everything they owned. *Gone.*

And all those people.

A flash of severed body parts scattered over crimson-coated pavement flashed against the backdrop of my tightly sealed eyes. Firemen. An entire news crew. Innocent people.

How many had they killed?

Fuck.

It's all my fault.

I didn't realize I'd whispered it until I sensed Frost stiffen beside me. "Don't you dare fucking say that."

Finally, I met his eyes, unable to keep my own from welling. Frost's hard green gaze bored into me. He shook his head, jaw taut.

"It's true, isn't it?" I asked, my voice watery. "They were there for *me*. Not you. If I'd just stayed away maybe—"

"Shut up."

I narrowed my eyes at him, and the wetness rimming them halted before any true tears could fall. "But—"

"Don't do that. Don't blame yourself. I can't stand it when you cry," he trailed off, suddenly unable to look me in the eye. His face reddened and his hands balled atop the soft sheets. "If you want someone to blame, blame the fucker who painted the streets red with innocent blood and fire. *Blame Rafe*. He's the one who did this." He turned to meet my gaze again, and the hardness in his eyes softened. "Not you, Rosie."

I managed a sagging smirk and pulled one of his fisted hands into mine, closing it between my calloused palms. "Okay," I replied lamely, but I think we both knew it wasn't, and would never be again.

"Christ, woman," Frost all but growled at me, his husky voice strained. "We've been here for days waiting for you to wake up...we weren't even sure if you *would* wake up."

The pale skin around his eyes was stained a purplish-red, and I wondered when the last time he slept was. Judging by the look of him, it had to have been days. "I—"

He held up a hand to stop me. "And now you want to sit there and try to blame *yourself* for what happened?"

Frost leaned forward and drew me sharply into his muscled chest, crushing me to him almost painfully. His shoulders were trembling. He inhaled the scent of me and planted a rough kiss atop my head, still not letting go. "Just…" he began, but couldn't finish, swallowing hard so his throat bobbed against my temple. "Just let me hold you for a minute, okay?"

I nodded against his chest, nuzzling in deeper as I wrapped the arm untethered by an IV and plastic tube around his middle and allowed myself to *breathe*.

After a minute, or maybe a few, I broke the silence, needing him to know that I would do whatever I could to help them rebuild what was taken from them. "I have some money saved up," I told him, my voice muffled against his thin t-shirt. "It's yours. Fucking *all* of it. We can—"

Frost jerked back and ran a hand through his white-blond hair. He rolled his eyes at me. "No need," he said without further explanation, and I heard the muted sound of footfalls across the room. "It's already been taken care of."

Frost's bright green eyes narrowed on the figure entering and I turned to find Azrael standing in the door-way. He was put together in a tailored ensemble that made him look even sharper than he usually did, but his perpetually smooth russet brown hair was unkept. And the rims of deep color around his eyes and sallowness in his cheeks told me he hadn't been sleeping much either.

He sighed the moment he saw me sitting up in bed. "I thought I heard you cursing."

I smirked.

Then what Frost meant clicked in my mind and my gaze jerked between them. He couldn't mean that Azrael...

No way.

Azrael was paying to replace all their things?

I looked at my captor, incredulous. He nodded silently, answering my thoughts. I clamped my jaw shut, grinding my teeth.

"I guess I won't cut your head off, then," I muttered. "But you deserve it."

Azrael pursed his lips and moved into the room with his hands clasped behind his back until he was standing over me on the other side of the bed. A memory of his brother struck me, of him pressing his foul lips to mine in a forceful kiss right before he hit me so hard in the head that I've been out for days.

"Sit," I told Azrael, my throat going dry. That face looming over me wasn't helping right now. I was trying to soothe my heart rate and shaking limbs, not make them worse.

He's not *his brother.*

Looking pained, Azrael did as I asked and sat near the edge of the wide bed. I was grateful that, for once, he didn't take it upon himself to comment openly on my thoughts.

"Where are the others?" I asked with a quirked brow, wondering why neither of them had heard me.

"Ethan is downstairs," Azrael said. "He's blasting some horrid music in the sitting room where he's set up something of a makeshift lab."

My brow furrowed.

"He's trying to recreate the shit he made back in his lab. The, uh, the vampire sunblock potion shit or whatever you want to call it."

Oh.

"And Blake?"

"Asleep," Frost replied, squeezing my hand again. "He's been up sitting with you the longest. He damn near fell out of this chair a couple times before Ethan and I made him go to bed. He'll be out for at least a few more hours."

My heart gave a little twinge and I swallowed. "And where are we exactly?" I asked, this time posing the question to Azrael, who I assumed would have the explanation I was seeking.

Azrael ran a small edge of the soft white sheets between his fingers, not looking at me. "My home."

My face went slack, mouth falling ajar. I'd guessed as much. It was either that or some swanky castle hotel. Without thinking, I kicked him hard beneath the covers, my foot connecting with the solid plane of his upper thigh. An aching pain ricocheted up my calf all the way to my thigh. I winced, angry that kicking him probably caused me more grief than it did him. "You *asshole*," I grumbled, unapologetically. "You kept me in that stupid cave when you had *this place*. The fuck?"

A look of shock crossed Azrael's features, and I

wondered if he was more surprised at my outburst or that I'd kicked him.

"Oh, come on," I hissed when he didn't bother replying. "It's not like it hurt."

He inclined his head, agreeing.

I went to pull myself out of the covers when the IV tugged at my hand and I flinched. "Stupid fucking thing," I muttered and pulled it from my skin, tossing it off the side of the bed to hang limply beneath a mostly drained IV bag on a metal pole.

"You should rest," Azrael said haltingly, and I didn't miss how his mismatched eyes darted to the thin trail of blood dribbling down to my wrist from the tiny wound.

"Rest?" I almost laughed, peeling the covers back so I could sit up properly, and feeling every stiff muscle and ache as I did. "There isn't time for that. You saw what your psychotic brother did. He needs to be stopped."

"No shit," Frost interjected, his expression hardening back into his usual resting-I'll-kill-you-face. "But before we go running to our deaths, let me grab you something to eat. You look like a raisin."

I scowled at him.

"A super-hot raisin," he amended.

"How can you both be so calm about this?" I asked, my temper flaring. "What's the plan? Or do you even have one?"

Azrael sighed heavily and rose from the bed, removing the metal pole from the side and using it as a sort of leaning post.

"What the hell are you sighing about?" I demanded. *"You're* the one who let the bastard get away."

"It's not that simple, Rosie."

"Why not?"

"Because," Azrael grimaced, his head bowed and eyes darkening. "Raphael has an army of followers at his back. And even if he didn't, he's been sequestered in his tower since Baton Rouge. The thing is impenetrable."

"And he's still *building* that army," Frost added. "It grows every day. I've been tracking his movements. He's recruiting soldiers faster than you can blink."

We all knew what he wanted. Raphael didn't believe vampires should go back to being what they were before the curse changed them. In his foul mind, the Vocari race had been *improved* upon. Had been *exalted.* And should take its rightful place at the top of the food chain, effectively turning the rest of humanity into a multihued snack.

I shivered. "He's *insane.*" I shook my head, all my still-sluggish thoughts coalescing into one certain one. "Az," I said in as gentle of a voice as I could possibly muster, and the ancient vampire raised his head until our eyes met. "You can't save him," I implored Azrael to see reason.

I'd only had the misfortune to meet Raphael once, but there was no denying what I saw inside of him. *He's a monster.* "He needs to be put down."

Azrael blinked and a flash of sizzling fury raced across his features and gleamed like fire in his eyes before he growled and looked away. His body went rigid. In an exhalation of shaky breath, he replied in barely a whisper. "I know."

I wished he'd *known* that a few days ago when we could've fucking done something about it, but there it is. At least he's seen the light. His deranged sibling needs to die, and he may be the only vampire strong enough to do the job.

"Are you guys forgetting about the fucking *army* he has at his back? Deciding to kill the guy is one thing, actually being able to do it is something completely different."

"Hmmm," Azrael said pensively. The deep, throaty sound somehow making my insides squirm and my toes curl. *Ugh.* "Then I suppose we'll be needing an army of our own."

I remembered how Azrael appeared through the smoke and flames with an entourage of vampires at his back in the streets of Baton Rouge and my hope surged. "Do you have one?"

Azrael's face fell. "No. At least, not one large enough to match Raphael's. No where near as many vampires as we would need for a fair fight."

My brain reeled from the conversation, reality snapping into me like a cold wet *smack* across the face. We were talking about war. *Vampire war.* How fucked up is that?

Barely a week ago, I was plotting ways to kill Azrael and escape his hideout. Worrying about when I would get to see my guys next. Squirming impatiently as doctors and nurses took blood, hair, and marrow samples from my body.

Now…what?

Was I actually going to *trust* Azrael?

I considered him from my seat on the soft mattress, tracing the planes of his face. He caught me watching him and his lips parted. I shut up my thoughts and locked them away, not wanting him to hear.

The answer to my question, it seemed, was *yes.* I was going to trust him. Because I didn't have any other choice. I'd already broken all my other rules. Why not this one, too? Why not break them all?

Azrael watched me curiously and I cleared my throat, glancing away from him and back to Frost.

"Then we build one," Frost says before I have a change to arrange my thoughts into coherent words. "If that's the only way, then that's what we'll do. I already knew a few who would join us."

I snorted. "What vampire in their right mind would rally behind a vampire standing next to the Black Rose?"

I was still laughing at the idea when I caught Azrael's slowly spreading grin. I wasn't sure I'd ever seen him smile before. It was…unsettling on a face that was usually so severe. And the sinful gleam in his eyes wasn't helping the effect. "They will if we can give them the sun."

CHAPTER 2

By the look on Azrael's face, I thought he was going to break into hysterical, maniacal laughter, but we were saved by a startled Ethan gasping in the doorway.

Ethan's handsome face went slack with relief when he saw me sitting up in bed. He was holding something up triumphantly in his hand as though it was a holy grail, but it was momentarily forgotten as he rushed into the room, stuffing the vial into Azrael's hands as he came to me.

He crawled onto the bed, took my face between his warm hands and wordlessly kissed me. His lips pressed against mine, softly at first, testing my strength. To make sure I wasn't going to shatter. When I deepened the kiss, an ache spread low in my belly. Ethan was all too eager to increase the pressure of his kiss, and his palms on my cheeks tightened.

A throat cleared somewhere behind him, and I almost whimpered when he pulled away, wanting to clutch him back to me. Wanting him to keep kissing me like I was the most precious thing in the world. Wanting to do a hell of a lot more than just *kiss* him now...

A warmth spread between my thighs and I tried to get my body under control while wishing Azrael would give me some alone time with Frost and Ethan. I could think of a few things I'd like to—

"Have you done it?" Azrael asked, breathless as he held the vial up to the light, his face paling.

Ethan gripped my hand tightly before he turned back to face Azrael. He wound his fingers through mine, and I wasn't sure he would be letting go anytime soon. Not that I minded. I didn't want him to.

"I did. But..." he paused. "I'll need more samples if we're going to be able to make more. That was all I could distil from what you gave me."

I shuddered, knowing that by *samples* he meant *more pieces of Rose.* But I was glad he didn't say it. I mean, I would give them all the blood they needed if it meant putting an end to Raphael and his merry band of murderous followers.

I'd killed hundreds of vampires, most of whom I prayed deserved it. But if we succeeded in this, there would be hundreds more dead. Exactly the kind I usually hunted. There would be *hundreds* less leeches out there ruining families and killing for sport. The idea was more than I could've dreamed of a few weeks ago. Hell, I may even put myself out of work.

But I doubted that. As long as there were supernatural

creatures in this world, there would need to be someone to keep them in check.

Azrael's adams apple bobbed in his throat. "And you're certain?" he asked dispassionately. "It's the same as what you and the others needled into your skin?"

I could tell by the crease in Azrael's brow, and the flaring of his cheekbones as he clenched his jaws together, that he was working hard to conceal some emotion from us. And by the way his stare was boring into Ethan's, I knew he was ransacking Ethan's mind for even the slightest hint of doubt.

"I'm sure," was Ethan's stony reply. "Will you go alone?"

My eyes widened, finally understanding.

Azrael was going to meet the sun for the first time in over a thousand years.

"There isn't enough there for all of us," Frost said in a low voice tainted with the sound of disappointment.

"Has it worn off already?" I asked, curious.

Ethan nodded. "Yeah, it started wearing off a couple days ago, and by yesterday it was gone from our systems entirely."

I bit my lower lip. *Shit.* I'd been really hoping it would last longer—of that one dose would be all it took, but I guess that wasn't the case. "I can give you more—"

"Not yet," Ethan interrupted with a gentle smile. "When you're fully healed."

Azrael was still contemplating the vial in his hands, holding it as though he was afraid it may vanish entirely if he wasn't staring directly at it. "I'll go with you," I said, surprising myself.

By the furrowed brows on Frost and Ethan, I could tell they were just as surprised at what I said as I was.

He was still a total dickhead, and I still didn't fully trust him. I wouldn't ever, I didn't think. But Azrael had come when we needed him. He'd saved me *and* my guys. And obviously he hadn't harmed them while I'd been asleep. In fact, other than tired, listless eyes, they looked to be in more than perfect health.

This was about more than my freedom, or what my blood could do anymore. After seeing what Raphael could do without remorse—killing all those people...

Well, I'd keep my word and help Azrael concoct a longer-lasting elixir to allow my guys to walk in sunlight, but we had bigger fish to fry now. We all knew it.

Azrael cocked his head at me, considering my offer. "If you catch fire, I'll be ready with a hose," I said lightly with a smirk and a wink, not wanting to make this any more awkward than it already was.

Az ran his tongue over his teeth and pulled his lower lips between them, biting down. "That would be...appreciated," he replied tentatively. "But I'm not sure you're well enough—"

I swung my legs from the bed and stood. My head teetered with a gripping sensation of vertigo for a moment before it subsided, and I caught myself with a widened stance. "See? Totally fine."

"Alright. But I'll have Amala tend to your wounds first. Camden, would you mind?"

I sensed Frost bristle at the use of his given name. No one called him that except his mother. His face soured as he rose, pushing off from his knees to stand and cross the room. "Yeah. I'll get her."

"Am I missing something? Who's Amala?"

I'd been asking Azrael, but it was Ethan who replied. "A witch," he said. "A really strong one," he paused and traced the embroidered golden threads on the comforter, eyes downcast. "She's probably the only reason you're still alive."

"And she'd have had you fully healed by now if I didn't need her abilities elsewhere," Azrael added just as Frost re-entered the room with a woman in tow behind him.

She looked to me in her late-twenties or perhaps her early thirties. But, like Azrael, she had this ancient air about her. The feel of her presence wasn't like a shiver slinking down my spine so much as it was more *suffocating*. Like her energy was clogging the room and pressing down on me like a physical weight.

The woman—or *witch* called Amala was curvy, with smooth skin the color of wet sand and almond-shaped eyes that watched me with a predatory stare. She was beautiful, in the way that a jaguar is beautiful before it bares its teeth.

She didn't waste any time, wading past Azrael and Ethan to stand directly next to me beside the bed. She was taller than me, but only by a few inches.

Her eyes were a soft caramel color, like they were maybe once brown, but had been bleached by the passage of time. I wasn't even sure if she could see.

She reached out to me and in a knee-jerk reaction I flinched away.

"Amala won't harm you. She is under my employ and...an old friend."

"Ha!" Amala said, her face twisting into a sneer. "Friends don't work friends to the bone creating wards. Nor do they bring women to be healed after they've broken them," her tone was saucy and lilting with the hint of an accent I couldn't place.

Azrael smirked.

Amala lifted her hands and I waited, wide-eyed, my gaze darting from Azrael standing sentinel, to Ethan, to Frost who was standing behind Amala with his arms crossed—watching her like a hawk as though he didn't fully trust her either. And eventually, back to Amala herself.

The witch flicked her fingers through the air and shut her unnerving eyes. In the span of a blink, there was a wavering shape hovering where her fingers just were. Golden and shining. Glowing. A circular shape with a line down its heart. Hanging impossibly in empty space.

A strange smell like burning metal and cold stone permeated the air.

I gasped as it exploded, scattering its shimmering glow over my head like a veil. A small sound escaped my lips, but as the bits of magical dust seeped into my pores and spread through my blood, I sighed. The sensation was a little *itchy*...I couldn't think if that was the right word to describe it. But it was also warm and almost *comforting*.

The ache at the top of my skull dulled, and after a

moment faded entirely. The uncomfortable bruising on my back that was keeping my muscles tense there faded, too.

I stretched out my limbs and let out a long breath. There was still some tension. A few kinks. But I felt better than I had in *days.*

"Thank you," I breathed.

Amala's brows raised. "Don't mention in," she replied and turned away. "That's the best I can do for now," she added, turning back to speak to Azrael as she slowly crossed the room to the door, her long deep burgundy dress dragging against the carpet. "She'll need to eat and drink to finish her recovery."

Azrael merely nodded in response but called after her before she could vanish from view. "And the wards?"

Amala stopped but did not turn. "They'll hold," she replied.

"How long?"

"For as long as they need to—so long as I still draw breath."

Azrael looked as though a massive weight had been lifted from his shoulders. "Thank—"

"Save it," Amala interrupted him, tilting her head to glare in his direction. I saw something dark cross her face. "You owe me for this, Azrael."

"I know."

She left a moment later and my shoulders sagged as the tension in the room left with her. "She's a real ray of sunshine, isn't she?"

Nobody laughed.

"Shall we?" Azrael intoned with an arm extended as though he expected me to thread mine through it. I walked past his crooked arm and out into the hall, leaving him and the others to trail behind me.

I had no idea where I was going and when I stepped out of the room into a corridor lined with doors and paintings and what looked to be a hallway on each end and a third going somewhere else from the middle, I stopped. I let Azrael pass me and lead the way as I fell into step between Frost and Ethan.

Ethan threaded his fingers through mine again, and Frost followed along just behind us.

We turned down the center hall and toward a long staircase leading down, following it until the floor leveled out again. We came into an open area with a stately dining room to our left and what looked like a sitting room but was now a makeshift laboratory to our right.

"I'll go get you something to eat," Frost grunted while cutting Azrael a warning glare.

Azrael, looking amused, said nothing. He waited, twisting the vial between his thumbs and forefingers at his front. "Did you manage to get the equipment you needed to administer it?"

It took me a moment to remember that the serum Ethan invented from my blood had to be tattooed into the skin.

"The gun is old—I got it at a twenty-four-hour pawn shop yesterday, but it should do the trick."

Azrael followed Ethan into the lab and sat in the

rolling stool Ethan nudged toward him, placing the vial back into Ethan's outstretched hand with a grimace.

"Any preference?" Ethan asked as he pulled on a pair of gloves and poured the contents of the vial into the little pot attached to the gun. The focused look he got in his eyes as he got everything prepared and then sat, straddling a stool was a massive turn on.

I licked my lips, moving in closer to watch.

Azrael shrugged and reached up behind his head to remove his shirt in one pull. I held my breath and clamped my jaw shut as his toned torso was exposed. Why did someone who was practically the devil have to look so much like a goddamned angel? My inner lioness purred at the broad expanse of his shoulders. The narrowing of his toned waist as it vanished into the waistband of his loose fitted jeans. The twin dimples in his back as he spun the stool, exposing his back to Ethan. "Doesn't matter," he replied, and I wondered if he wanted it on his back so he wouldn't have to look at the same image every day for another thousand years.

Ethan's eyes sparked with mischief and Azrael flinched, shoving the stool away before Ethan could bring his tattooing needle close enough to his flesh. *"Don't,"* Azrael warned. "If you ink a cock into my skin, I'll have yours for breakfast."

Ethan paled and unable to help myself, I burst into tear-filled laughter. The image of the great and terrible Azrael with an enormous dick inked into his back too much to handle.

I wiped a stray tear from my cheek and settled,

catching my breath. "Fuck," I said between breaths. "I didn't know you swung that way, Az."

"There's a lot you don't know," he retorted, his voice a low-pitched grumble.

My face must have registered my shock. It wasn't the response I'd been expecting.

He arched a brow at me.

"You mean you..." I trailed off, unable to ask him outright.

Azrael grumbled something I didn't catch and moved back toward Ethan, this time turning to give Ethan access to his chest. Smart man.

Ethan, carefully this time, with the tips of his ears stained pink, moved in closer to the ancient vampire. I could see the gears and cogs turning behind his steeped tea eyes.

Azrael shook his head twice before nodding, and I realized Ethan was creating images in his mind for Azrael to decide from. *Ugh*. How was he so comfortable with Azrael being inside his head? Just the thought that Az might be listening in on my thoughts at any given moment made my insides squirm.

No one needed to know me on that personal of a level. My thoughts weren't exactly *pure*.

"Az?" Azrael asked and it took me a moment to realized he was responding to my thoughts and wondering at the newly minted nickname. I'd used it earlier too, hadn't I? I didn't realize it, but then I suppose he hadn't either straight away. *Azrael* was just such a mouthful.

I rolled my eyes. "Would you *please* stay the fuck out of my head, Azrael?"

"I like it," he said, not wincing even a tiniest bit as Ethan's tattoo needle bit into his flesh. "*Az.*"

I growled.

"If you want me to stay out of your head, you'll just have to learn to make me."

I groaned again, louder this time. Azrael had already begun training me how to withstand his compulsion, and how to erect walls in my mind to keep him out, but I'd barely managed to evict him for more than a few seconds before it felt like my head was going to explode from the pressure of his attack. "I tried that, remember?"

He reached up to shove his hair back away from his face and the veins in his bicep thickened with the movement, defining an already defined muscle.

"You'll need to try harder."

I crossed my arms. There was no way I'd ever beat him at his own game. He was too much older. Stronger. It was useless.

"It's not useless," Azrael said. "Your mother once bested my brother."

I dropped my gaze. I still wasn't sure if I fully believed that. "It's true," Az continued. "Believe it or not, you have the capacity to be stronger of mind than I could ever dream to be. I'm surprised you yourself can't read thoughts yet. If the rumors are to be believed, Andora— your ancestor—she could by the time she was sixteen. Perhaps sooner."

"Wait," I said, uncomprehending. "You're saying *I* can read minds, too?"

"You should be able to. Or, at least, I thought you would."

"But my mother couldn't."

"Are you sure?"

I had to think about it. She did have this way of always seeming to know what I was going to say before I even said it, but I honestly thought that was just a mother's intuition. "No," I finally replied, because I wasn't sure. But I couldn't understand why she wouldn't have told me.

Thinking about it now, though, I thought I knew.

It made me disgustingly uncomfortable knowing Azrael could read my thoughts at any time. Without my knowledge. It would have been less awful if it was my mom, sure, but it still would have cleaved a rift between us.

There are some things—hell, *lots of things* you don't want your mother knowing you're thinking about when you're in your early teens. If Azrael was right, she didn't tell me because she didn't want me to feel uncomfortable around her.

All we had in the world was each other. We moved around a lot while I was young and didn't understand why. And when we settled in Silverton and I met the guys and mom told me about our ability...and about the vampires...I stopped making friends. Unable to connect with another human being in the same way after knowing I was so different to them.

That they wouldn't ever understand.

"Thought so," Azrael said, his eyes with that faraway look they got sometimes when he was remembering something in his own past. Like looking at a photograph with fondness for the memory it contains, but also pain for the loss of its happiness.

What happened to you? I thought, not for the first time.

Azrael snapped out of his trance-like state and cleared his throat. "You about done?" he asked Ethan, his tone suddenly bored.

"Just about," Ethan said and then lifted the needle a second later. "There."

I moved around to get a better look and found a tribal sort of sun inked into the toned flesh of Azrael's left breast. It was fitting, I suppose, but also lacking in so much creativity.

Azrael arched a brow at me. "Fine, then you pick next time," he hissed and tugged his shirt back on, not caring that he was staining it with small droplets of his own blood and leftover ink.

"With pleasure," I murmured. "Someone has to save you from unoriginality."

Azrael rose from the stool while Ethan put away his used gear. For the tiniest second, I thought I saw his hand tremble at his side, but I blinked, and it was still as a surgeon's, leaving me to wonder if I'd imagined it.

"Ready?" I asked, trying to sort out where the exit of this massive house was.

"Wait," Ethan called, pulling off his plastic gloves with little sucking sounds to lift a pair of aviator sunglasses from the top of an antique side table pushed against the wall. "Here," he said, handing them to Azrael. "You might need these. It really is blinding at first. Felt like my retinas were going to evaporate the first time."

…and Ethan had only been without the sun for a little over a year. Azrael hadn't seen anything like it in over a *thousand* years.

Fuck.

Azrael took the proffered sunglasses with a blank stare, clenching them in his fist. He didn't thank Ethan, but by the strain in his eyes I thought it was mostly because he was thinking about a million other things.

"It's this way," he said finally, gesturing to the hallway leading down past the dining room. He turned and left without another word and I tossed Ethan an impish grin over my shoulder before I went to follow Azrael.

He led me down a short staircase and through another corridor that brought us past a kitchen where I saw Frost whispering with an older woman in a white apron—three pots simmering on the stove in front of them. My stomach twisted at the rich smell of homemade chicken soup.

I hoped it was almost ready because I was fucking ravenous. Fully cooked or not, I had every intention to eat the whole freaking pot when we got back inside.

My mouth watered as we turned down one last hallway and I could see a large wooden door, at least eleven feet tall and four feet wide sealing off the entrance. The windows next to it were shuttered with the same heavy metal shutters as I'd seen in the room awoke in upstairs.

Not a hint of sunlight poured through anywhere. Only a dimly glowing chandelier in the wide entryway lit the space. "You know, I wasn't kidding about the hose," I half joked. "If there's, like, a garden entrance maybe we should use that in case I have to douse you."

Azrael didn't laugh.

"If I were to burn, it would be a small mercy," he murmured, so quietly I wasn't even sure I heard him right.

"Do you want me to...?" I pointed at the door, feeling more than a little awkward and wanting to badly to go back to hating him. It was easier than whatever was happening right now.

Azrael, my captor, was allowing me to escort him *outside*. Where, if he burned, I could run away. Not that I would because my guys were still inside. Oh, and that was another thing. He'd *saved* not only me, but my guys, too.

And now we were...

What?

Working together?

I still couldn't wrap my head around it.

Azrael finally nodded, and I stepped forward as he braced himself in front of the wide wooden pane, putting on the sunglasses Ethan gave him.

There were three locks and a deadbolt on the door, and I took my time undoing each one until all that remained was to twist the handle and pull it open.

A small pang in my gut surprised me just before I did and the silent plea for him *not* to burn caught me off guard. Why should I care?

Shaking myself, I reefed the door open in one quick

movement and the golden hues of evening sunlight spilled into the room. It was bright, even for my eyes, but Azrael's hiss of pain told me it was even more painful for him—even with the sunglasses on.

But...he didn't burn.

My shoulders relaxed and I ran a hand over the back of my neck where an annoying prickle had formed.

Azrael stood facing the sun expressionless. Motionless. Speechless.

"Az?"

No reply.

I didn't realize just how pale he was until now. Where his skin was exposed on the curse of his elbow and his forearms—on his neck and his face, it was...

Well, it was like sunlight reflecting off snow. I damn near had to shield my eyes. "*Damn,* Az," I muttered. "I think we need to get you a spray tan, you're burning my eyes."

When he didn't so much as smirk at my attempted humor, I gulped and walked nearer. I touched his arm and he flinched but didn't move away. I dropped my hand. "Do you..." I brushed my long dark hair back from my face, mildly grossed out by how oily it felt. I needed a shower. Badly. "Do you want to go outside?"

He didn't answer me, but his lips parted, and he glanced down at himself, as though coming out from a trance or a very vivid dream surprised to find himself still intact.

Azrael stepped to the threshold and dragged in a

halting breath. I had a little trouble breathing too when I saw what awaited us on the other side of the door.

A marble staircase lead out to a lush garden blooming with at least two dozen different plants and flowers I couldn't name. And further, there laid a verdant valley drenched in the golden light of the slowly setting sun. Beyond that crouched a copse of sparse trees on a gently sloping hill that fell away to reveal the shimmering gleam of the ocean disappearing into the distance.

Where the hell are we?

The air was a bit humid and the scents of warm wood, briny sea, and pollenating flora filled my nose. It looked like something out of a story book. Like the garden of Eden. All that was missing was the…

Nope. There it is. A massive gnarled apple tree that looked as though it had to be at least two hundred years old. With withering black bark and sun-stained leaves. A single shining crimson apple hanging heavily from the left side. The sun playing with the color to make it look almost like it was on fire.

Huh.

If that's the forbidden fruit, then is Azrael supposed to be Adam or the Devil?

My breath caught when I turned back to him to find him standing rigid just outside the door, his hands hard fists against his sides. His face a mask of stone save for the single tear falling down to his jaw from the edge of his sunglasses.

"Azrael," I started, unsure what to say. My own chest tight with emotion. I hadn't expected this.

He huffed, angling his head away from me, and when he spoke, his voice was gravellier than usual. "You can go."

"It's fine. I'll stay."

Truth be told, I was enjoying the sunshine and the fresh air a lot more than I thought I would. I spotted a little table in the garden with two chairs. Worn wrought iron and more a decoration than anything, but, "Why don't I bring my lunch out here and we could—"

"*Go*," he growled, and the grating sound of the command made my skin bristle.

I wasn't about to argue with that voice. I'd only heard him use it once before and I knew it was a dangerous tone he used only when he was really serious.

I fled back into the house and turned back to see his massive body slump to the ground and begin to shake before the door clicked shut, sealing me off from him.

CHAPTER 3

*A*ll of them refused to touch me before I'd eaten and showered. I would be insulted, but I knew they were doing it for my benefit and not their own. They wanted me properly nourished and feeling myself again before they soiled me with their welcome dirty deeds.

Blake just about crushed me when he finally awoke just an hour after I ate lunch. Shoving through Ethan and Frost as they circled like worried mother hens. Apparently, there was still some lingering worry about my brain injury, but after I'd reassured them seven times that I felt completely *fine*, they finally bought it and took a step back.

So, I did what any woman craving the feel of her lovers' touch would do and I stuffed my face as quickly as I possible could without giving myself a mad stomachache. Then I rushed into the massive bathroom down the hall from my bedroom and stripped so I could take the quickest shower of my life.

As much as I yearned to linger under the caress of the warm silky water and luxuriate in the plethora of intoxicating soaps and shampoos and oils and creams, I wanted my guys more.

Way more.

They were ready for me when I came out of the washroom in a plume of jasmine scented steam. The room was warm despite my skin still being heated from the shower. Or maybe it was the sight of their three naked bodies that was making body warm.

The metal shutter on the window that'd been there earlier was retracted now and the glow of moonlight painted the plum carpet in cloud-dappled shadows. It cast my guys in varying shades of deep gray and stark white, playing with the planes of their bodies, emphasizing each and every muscle.

I resisted the urge to look outside, wanting to check and see if Azrael was still in the place I'd left him just outside the front door. If I looked straight down, I'd be able to see him from here.

But it wasn't my concern. None of my damned business.

I didn't care.

I *don't* care.

Lifting my chin, I had the divine satisfaction of watching Blake, Ethan, and Frost's expressions as I dropped my towel to the carpet and felt my nipples harden.

I licked my lips. "Who's first?"

Frost stepped forward and I grinned, pulling my lower

lip between my teeth. "Scratch that," I said, and he quirked a brow at me. "I want *all* of you. *Now.*"

I couldn't imagine *not* having all of them. How could I choose who went first? I wanted to feel each of their bodies pressed into mine. Especially after everything that'd happened. It struck me just how close I came to losing them. I had to shove down the swell of agony surging up to swell in my throat at the thought.

You didn't lose them, though, I told myself. *And now you're going to show them how grateful you are that they're all still here.* Vampire or not. They were *alive,* and I would never let anything happen to them again. Not for as long as I was still living, and after that, I could only hope that they'd be strong enough to fend for themselves.

"Are you sure?" Ethan asked, the tips of his ears going pink. I considered him, and his mammoth cock already mostly hard below his navel.

I licked my lips again, wanting to wrap them around it —to feel his length and girth fill my mouth and press against the back of my throat.

"*So* fucking sure," I replied, my breaths deepening.

Frost moved in a blur of solid muscle and a shock of white-blond hair until he had me roughly scooped up into his arms and then deposited me in a small toss onto the massive bed. I bounced a bit, giggling. My cheeks hurt from the strain of my wide grin and I couldn't seem to make it stop.

This was fucking happiness.

This was bliss.

I'd been missing out for so many years.

Then I guess you have years *to make up for,* the feisty little minx cooed in the back of my mind, spreading her legs with a come-hither stare and a crooked finger.

I had no fucking idea how I was going to have them all at once, but when Blake moved in and stole a rough kiss from my lips, making my back arch and a surprised little moan claw up my throat, I realized I didn't care.

My hands fisted greedily into Frost's hair as he trailed kisses down my belly. And Ethan made my body erupt into tiny shivers as he breathed warmly against my neck, brushing pillow-soft kisses down to my collarbone.

My pussy was already slick with silky wetness and it felt like an inferno was coiling down through my core, making my thighs squeeze as Frost made his way to the mound of my sex. He pressed his hot lips against the spot just above my clit and then flicked his tongue out, tasting me. I whimpered into Blake's mouth and he gripped me hard by the jaw, forcing my lips back to his when my moans broke us apart.

His tongue slithered into my mouth and when Frost flicked his tongue again, I thought I might explode from all the sensations skittering like rogue shockwaves over my skin.

Ethan lifted my body from the bed, putting himself beneath me. All the while Blake held tight to my jaw, forcing me to keep kissing him, and Frost never ceased the teasing flicks of his tongue.

My body was horizontal with Ethan's, and I could feel the hard press of his cock against the base of my spine. His hands came around my middle, trailing upward until they cupped my breasts, kneading and pinching gently until I was shivering in ecstasy.

Frost's hand brushed my opening and I convulsed at the roaring need in my veins. I was *aching* for the pressure of his fingers inside me, but he wasn't priming to push them into me. Breaking apart from Blake for an instant, I saw that his fist was now wrapped securely around Ethan's cock between my legs, bringing him to a full head.

Ethan trembled beneath me and his breaths came hot against my ear.

"Look at me," Blake whispered, and I turned to find his dark eyes boring into me. "That's it," he crooned. "Keep those beautiful amber eyes on me."

"Slow," Ethan warned, and I barely had time to register what Frost was doing before a warm, soft liquid dripped down between my cheeks and Frost pressed the tip of Ethan's massive cock into my ass.

I sucked in a breath and Blake wrapped his hand around the back of my neck, gripping me there to keep my eyes focused on his. To keep my head raised without my needing to put in the effort of holding it up myself.

Ethan eased slowly in and out, going a little further each time. I truly didn't think he would fit, but after a few moments of discomfort, he was fully inside me and I groaned against Blake's lips as he pressed them to mine once more, then moved his mouth lower, kissing the spit just below my jaw, setting my blood ablaze.

Bite me. Bite me. Bite me.

Fuck!

"T-take it," I managed, quaking and moaning as Frost

helped me rock against Ethan's cock in my ass, bringing me ever closer to climax.

Blake stilled and I watched his gaze flicker to Frost, as though asking the ringleader for permission.

There was a moment of tense silence, where only the sounds of my stilted moans filled the chamber, before Frost nodded. "But only a little. She's still healing."

I licked my lips, my skin buzzing with anticipation.

"When I say," Frost commanded as Blake leaned in and I obligingly tipped my head to one side in Blake's hand and he pressed his thumb tight against my carotid, feeling the strong pulse there. Blake's fangs slid free of his gums and his dark eyes glittered with suspense.

I was so close to cumming. Ethan was shaking beneath me, his hands on my breasts warming and his breaths at my ear getting harder, and faster.

Frost moved in closer between both mine and Ethan's legs, settling himself low with knees spread out against the sheets.

Oh shit.

"You tell me if this is too much," he growled, his own fangs dropping low to stipple his lower lip. He fanned a hand over my lower belly and wrapped his hand around his cock, flicking the tip of it over my opening.

I moaned loudly at the sensation, my body coming alive with a raw, animal need.

"Please," I whimpered, realizing what he meant to do and wanting him to get the fuck on with it. If I didn't come soon, I was going to fucking pass out from all the shaking with need. Already there were a few dark spots clinging to the edges of my vision as my body ached for climax.

Ethan slowed his thrusts from behind and I almost cried out, but he was only slowing so Frost could enter me, too. Frost inched inside my pussy slowly at first, and when he met no resistance and I made it abundantly clear with my near-screaming moans that there was no pain, he thrust in the rest of the way and shouted, "Now!"

I gasped as I felt the blissful fullness of both Ethan and Frost inside me at once, just as Blake clamped down on my artery, his fangs sinking deep into my skin. The pain ebbed in a matter of second and made way for wave after wave of blinding pleasure.

I wanted to cry at the force of it. At this feeling of absolute fullness. And not just in the physical sense. This joining of us all was what my body and soul had been aching for since I first laid eyes on them all again. Our puzzle of four souls was complete and there couldn't be anything else in this whole godforsaken world that could ever feel more right.

I was dizzy with the injection of Blake's venom, a mass of clenching skin and shattering pleasure.

As Ethan and Frost began to move, one thrusting in, while the other pulled slightly out, both pumping into me at the same, but opposite times, I thought I was going to explode.

I was going to unravel and be left a pile of whimpering flesh against the sheets.

I felt the climax begin and chased it to its apex. My moans grew louder, as did Blake's groaning against my throat, Ethan's breaths against my ear, and Frosts grunts as he slammed harder into me—his thumb moving low to circle my wet clit, spurring me on faster to the edge.

"Come for us Rose," Frost roared, and the command all but undid me.

Blake wrapped a hand around my throat, just above where he still suckled slowly near the nape of my neck, putting a small amount of pressure on my airway.

I came like I'd never come before. The climax spiraling so hard through my body that I thought I'd be torn apart by the force of it. Ethan came with me, his already rock-hard body turning to shuddering stone beneath me. Our bodies slippery with sweat.

Frost kept on through my climax, pushing it to go on longer, the dual sensation of him inside me and his thumb meticulously stroking my clit threw me into a second orgasm before the first could even properly finish and Blake let up on my airway, allowing me a hard breath that made my head spin as I shouted obscenities long and loud into the steamy air.

Frost came with me this time, his hand on my belly and the other wrapped tightly around the back of my thigh clenching tightly as he groaned, thrusting his last.

"*Fuck*," he bellowed, bowing his head at the force of his ecstasy just as Blake released his fangs from my neck and stared into my eyes, his own glazed and drooping as I realized he'd been coming with us, stroking his own proud length as he'd drunk from me.

Blake set my head down against Ethan's shoulder and my golden-haired knight nuzzled into my neck as he wrapped his arms possessively around my middle, enveloping me in his warmth. I melted into him, completely shattered. If my heart was beating any faster, it would hammer a hole right through my chest.

My eyelids fluttered as both Ethan and Frost eased their way out of me. "That's it," whispered Ethan, turning my body so I was on my side with his arms still wrapped around me, his chest pressed against my back.

Frost appeared in front of me, brushing the sweat-dampened long black hair from my face. "Rest," he said, hushing me when I tried to argue.

My consciousness wavered and before I knew it, with the warmth of Ethan wrapped protectively around me, Frost's whispered demands, and Blake crooning some melody I just faintly recognized, I was falling into a deep, sublime sleep.

Even as unconsciousness took me, my smile remained.

I didn't think it would ever fade.

CHAPTER 4

I tip-toed out of the room barefoot, in nothing but the bathrobe I'd found in the adjoining bathroom the night before. The guys were all still asleep. A puddle of hot man flesh on my bed. I could get used to the sight of that...

Blake was the only one who stirred as I disentangled myself from them, which was funny, because he was the only one *not* tangled up with us, instead he slept alone at the edge of the mattress. The movement was enough to wake him and for him to shoot an arm out to roughly grab me by the wrist, stopping me from leaving.

I kissed him softly, softening his wide eyes back to sleepy ones while I mouthed *water* to reassure him that I would be right back. He relaxed his hold and I was able to wriggle out of his grasp and pad to the door.

I found my way through the maze of corridors and stairways to the kitchen I'd seen only yesterday, where I'd gone to fetch the biggest bowl of hearty chicken noodle soup ever to fit in the stomach of a human being after leaving Azrael outside.

I had no idea what time it was, but it was still dark, and the windows were open, so I had to guess it was the middle of the night, sometime at least an hour before the start of sunrise. I had to assume the shutters were on some kind of timer.

"Oh dear!" The exclamation caught me so by surprise that I jumped and let loose a small chirp as I spun.

"Estelle?" Her round eyes took me in from her spot behind an island table. Her hands were poised over a mound of dough, flour caked into the wrinkles of her knuckles and palms.

She snapped out of her surprise and glanced at a clock on the wall I hadn't noticed before. I followed her gaze to find it was a little after three-thirty in the morning. "What are you doing up—"

I crossed the eight feet of space between us and wrapped her up in a hug, feeling her stiffen in response. "I'm so happy you're alright," I managed before awkwardly stepping back.

The glow of last night's affair with my guys was making me soft, I realized. I never would have hugged her otherwise. I cleared my throat, searching for an explanation that would make sense.

"I thought Azrael might have..." I trailed off.

It *had* crossed my mind. That the reason why Estelle wasn't here was because Azrael had gotten 'rid' of her. It's pained me to think it, but like so many other painful things in my life, I'd shoved the thought away. Locked it tightly in a little box in the back of my mind and promptly forced myself to forget about it.

In a world of blood and monsters, there wasn't any room for softness and saints. At least, not if you wanted to survive.

A tiny stab of guilt pinched my gut. Not for the first time, I wondered at how much trouble I'd gotten my guys into. And how much trouble I'd made for myself in the process. I had no doubt that they would be my undoing. My love for them would destroy me.

But hell...it was too late to do anything about it now.

Burn bright, mom used to say. I didn't think she meant burn hot and fast and die young like all the rest of my ancestors, but you know...minor details.

"Well of course I'm alright," Estelle tutted, pressing her flour-caked palms back into the dough. "It's like you think him the devil incarnate, girl."

I lifted a brow. I knew Azrael wasn't as awful as my mind originally made him out to be, but... he was still Azrael. He still took me hostage, nearly killed my guys, and the fire I sometimes glimpsed within him spoke of a fury I could only ever dream of understanding.

A fury that'd been simmering for a thousand years.

"What are you making?" I asked, changing the subject.

She cocked her head at me. "Don't tell me you didn't know bread starts as a great glob of dough?"

I chuckled.

"I'm making biscuits to have with breakfast," she explained. "Why? Are you hungry already?"

I did feel the beginning of hunger in my gut, but it wasn't so bad yet.

"I'll be needing another couple of hours to have anything ready," she added before I could respond.

Shaking my head, I strolled over to where there was a coffee machine, a big full pot of steaming brewed beans ready for the taking. "That's okay," I told her. "Coffee and water are all I was after."

"Be a dear and make me one, too, would you," Estelle said, her brows drawing inward as she focused on putting all her strength into turning and pressing on the dough ball. "Cream is in the fridge," she said between grunts. "It's just there, blendin' in with the other cupboards."

I found it after a couple tries and pulled out the creamer while I flipped the lid off a little porcelain pot of sugar. "How do you take it?"

"Just a lump of sugar," she said as she turned the dough into a metal bowl and set to covering it with a damp cloth. "But I like it white as milk."

I wrinkled my nose but made it like she said. "Won't it be cold with all that cream?" I asked her as I set the mug down next to her at the sink where she was scrubbing her hands with a little white-bristled brush.

"I don't much like coffee," she explained, drying her fingers on a tea towel and lifting the mug of coffee-stained cream to her thin lips. "But I need it to keep up to all that needs doing."

"You know I'd be happy with some toasted Eggos and syrup, right?" I asked with a raised brow. "And I'd *also* be fine to make it myself."

"What on earth is an Eggo?"

She couldn't be serious? Christ, how long had Azrael had her under his spell? "It's a pre-made waffle. They come frozen in a box and you pop them into a toaster to warm them before you eat them."

Estelle made a face of disgust and wetted a cloth to start cleaning the flour off the countertops. "That sounds terrible."

"Compared to your cooking, I guess they are."

She glowed at the compliment but seemed to be trying to hide it. She coughed a little to conceal her discomfort and said, "You'd best get back to bed. If you stay in here talking my ear off, I'll never get anything done."

I wanted to tell her she looked like she was doing just fine since I came in, but I stopped myself. "Okay," I said, more chipper as the coffee worked its way into my veins. "See you in a while."

She waved me off without looking and went to the fridge to pull out some ingredients for god knows what. I grinned to myself as I left the kitchen, thinking to myself that for a woman compelled, she had quite the personality.

I WANDERED THE MANSION FOR WHAT FELT LIKE AN HOUR AS I drained my coffee and went back twice to bother Estelle for two more and a few glasses of water. I had a good lay of it now, I thought.

It had to be at least ten-thousand square feet. If not more. And there were older looking doors that seemed to be sealed off. The old iron latches on them fused from the passage of time. So, really, it could have been a lot larger than I thought, depending on what lay behind all those doors at the back of the castle-like house.

After my stroll, I found myself wondering where Azrael was. I'd been into every room in the house, I was sure of it. And I hadn't found him. Or any of his lackeys. There was one girl sleeping in a room on the top floor—the one who I'd seen in the kitchen the day before, but other than my guys and me and Estelle, the place seemed to be empty.

It was as I was passing by the front door for the second time that I considered the possibility that he'd never come back inside.

I set my mug down on a small side table near the door and bit my lip, wondering if I should even look. If he would just make me leave again if he was even out there.

But, telling myself that I wanted some fresh air regardless, I convinced myself to push the door open and step outside. Azrael wasn't where I'd left him on the landing and I sighed, unsure if it was disappointment or relief I was feeling.

The sky was well on its way to brightening now. The moon still hung heavy and near-full in the dark sky, but the deep navy was giving way to splashes of purple and little rays of pinkish light as the sun crept up to the horizon.

A peaceful warm breeze lifted my hair and I inhaled the sweet and intoxicating scent of flowers waking to the coming sun. My skin bloomed with goosebumps at the crisp night.

I took in the gardens and turned, remembering there was a small table down among the foliage where I could sit.

That was where I found him.

Stock still with a solemn and slightly forlorn expression on his otherwise placid face. He didn't seem to have even noticed that I'd come outside. His gaze was fixed on the horizon, as though he could force the sun to rise again from sheer force of will.

"Hey," I ventured, stepping down to meet him in the garden.

He turned to me with glazed eyes. "Hmm?"

It was strange to see him so…what was the word?

Docile?

Soft?

Completely exposed?

"Azrael, are you okay?"

His eyes crinkled.

"You haven't been out here all night, have you?"

He blinked. "Yes. I think I have."

He still hadn't answered my first question, so I sat down opposite him, feeling the rough caress of rusted iron rake over the towel-like material of my bathrobe. "Everything okay?"

Azrael came back to himself in stages. The slackness of his expression tightening infinitesimally until he was back to looking like his usual brooding self, resting-murder-face and all.

"Thank you," he breathed, his jaw taut and flaring. For one heart-stopping second, I thought he may cry again, and I couldn't stomach the image of it. It was just so...*wrong*. Monsters don't cry.

"I've been a vampire—a *monster* for a thousand years, Rose. But I was once Vocari. The same as you."

I grimaced, choosing not to comment for fear I may say something to piss him off. "What are you thanking me for?" I asked, instead.

He waved a hand toward where the sun was just peeking over the horizon, washing the sky in shades of orange and pink and red. "This."

I watched his jaw work as he ground his teeth. "I truly thought I'd never see it again. Never *feel* it."

My chest felt suddenly heavy and I wrung my hands in the loose fabric of my robe, unable to look him in the eye. "It was just a bit of blood," I said. "And I think you'd have taken it from me whether I let you or not."

"Maybe," he replied. "I'm not sure what I would have done if you refused."

I pursed my lips. At least he was honest.

"But I know what others would do," he mused, sitting back in his seat, a pensive look on his ethereal face. "My brother may want to end you, but others—the ones who would do anything to walk in sunlight again—they would do worse."

I shuddered involuntarily and set my jaw to stave off the split second of fear. "Let them try."

Azrael smirked and I glowered at him. "What?" I demanded.

"Always so feisty. One day it's going to bite you in the ass."

My mouth fell open.

"Did you just say ass?"

He crooked a brow at me.

"You did," I accused. "You just swore."

He frowned and grunted, his face hardening. "You must be rubbing off on me."

I grinned wickedly.

Azrael rolled his eyes at my expression. "Now be quiet so I can watch the sun rise in peace."

I gave him all of ten seconds before I couldn't contain all the questions bubbling up to the surface anymore and they began to burst from my lips.

"What are we going to do about your brother?" I blurted. "Are we actually going to have to amass an army? That seems a bit extreme, doesn't it?"

Azrael sighed, his eyes never leaving the glowing ball of fire in the sky as it chewed a path into the clouds. "Desperate times call for—"

"*Really?* Do people actually say shit like that?"

He shrugged.

"Yes, Rose. We are going to build an army and then we are going to kill my brother," he paused, and his jaw twitched. "You were right; I am a, what was it you called me? A stupid *fucker mother*? Yes, that was it."

I blushed, vaguely remembering being unable to put my words in their right order after the blow to my head.

"I know he shouldn't be allowed to live. I've known it for a very long time."

ELENA LAWSON

I tried to understand what kept him from taking out the trash ages ago but had a hard time empathizing. I never had any siblings. And my last bit of family died with my mother. I never really knew my father, so the man might as well be dead, too.

But then...I imagined—however hard it was to imagine—that one of my guys turned dark. Became a monster like Raphael. I would like to think that I would put them out of their misery—end their madness. But I wasn't sure. And the uncertainty made me understand Azrael's tangled emotions a little better.

"He's family," I said, holding back the urge to tell him for the hundredth time that he's an idiot. "I...I get it."

"Do you?"

I winced. "No, actually," I said, but my tone was light. Almost joking. "Sorry, but I really don't. He's a fucking psycho, Az."

For once he didn't berate me for cursing. And he didn't disagree with me, either. He only said, in a voice so low I wasn't sure I heard him right. "He wasn't always."

And that was that.

We sat together in thick silence until the sun was fully up and the sky so bright it hurt my eyes to look at it, then Azrael turned to me and smiled softly, a spark of playfulness in his eyes that I'd never seen in him before.

This was one side of him. The light side that was substantially smaller than the dark one, but there it was. There *he* was. The Azrael who didn't want to compel me to do his bidding. The Azrael who was paying to repair and replace all my guys lost in Baton Rouge. The Azrael who saved all of our lives.

"Come on," he said and stood, holding out his hand to me.

I stared at it incredulously, and without even fully forming a decision, reached out and took it. Both exhilarated and a bit repulsed but suppressing the latter.

Azrael squeezed my hand and one corner of his full lips tipped up in a sly grin. "Time to draft us an army."

CHAPTER 5

"*W*ait, what's happening?" Frost demanded; his fists clenched at his sides like two blocks of porcelain cement.

"We're going to recruit an army," I told him, finishing up getting on all my gear. He was just mad that I didn't tell him until *after* I'd had my way with him.

When I came into the room to find Frost alone in my bed, the other two god knew where else in the massive house, I couldn't help myself.

His morning wood just too tempting to resist. And after he'd woken up find me straddling him, my pussy poised over his aching erection, he was all too happy to oblige me.

"You haven't even fully healed yet," he complained, tugging on a pair of jeans with a sour expression on his face.

I didn't want to have this fight *again*.

I'd already had it with Azrael this morning.

He wanted to take *my* guys with him to go collect vampires to rally to our side and *leave me here*.

As *fucking* if I was going to let that happen.

It took the better part of thirty minutes to convince Azrael to bring me along. We both knew I was a more apt fighter than my guys were—no offense to them, and that if Azrael was with us, we weren't in any real danger, anyway.

He could just compel any vamps that caused us trouble like he'd compelled all three of my guys at once back in Baton Rouge when he made them forget where his dank ass cave was.

"Azrael is coming," I said in a tone that I hoped conveyed that it was past the point of arguing. That he wouldn't win. "So just chill."

His nostrils flared and if his face got any more red, he might sprout roots and leaves and I'd have to start calling him tomato-head. "You're going to burst a blood vessel."

"You're never going to stop being a pain in my ass, are you?" he hissed, but the heat was already leeching out of his cheeks and his bright green gaze.

"Nope," I said with a pop of my lips. "Better get used to it."

"Just..." he said, throwing a hand through his white-blond hair. "Take it easy, okay?"

"Yes *dad*," I joked, and he whipped a towel at me, hitting me smack in the face.

I clawed it away and shoved it back at him, laughing.

Ethan came into the room a second later, smiling when he caught sight of me laughing. "What did I miss?"

"Just Frost being a dickhead."

"More like Rose being a stubborn ass, as usual."

Ethan made a sound like *mmm* and moved across the room to help me with the top part of my zipper in the back of my fighting leathers. He deftly zipped it the rest of the way and kissed the back of my head. I swallowed a blush before it could claw up my throat.

"I heard," he said, and I could hear the pride in his voice. "Azrael has been griping and moaning about how annoyingly tenacious you are for the past hour."

That just made me grin more.

"Why aren't you ready?" I asked, turning to inspect him. "We're leaving just after dark."

Which, if I had a good handle on the time now was in about an hour or so. And yet Ethan was still in a pair of sweats that did nothing to conceal the very prominent bulge and curve of his cock beneath. And he was barefoot. Wearing a threadbare t-shirt with an ink-stain near the hem.

His smile fell. "I'm staying," he replied. "I don't want to, but Azrael is right. If we're using the lure of sunlight to rally vampires to our side against Rafe, then we'll need to make good on our promise. Give them a little taste of it so they'll stay. So they'll be loyal."

I got what he was trying to say in not so many words. He needed to stay to create more of the serum.

And he would need more of my blood to do it.

He must have seen the bitter look on my face because he said. "I won't take any marrow. I know you hate that… Just a bit of blood should do the trick. We just want to give them a taste, so they'll stay. They need to earn any more than that."

From the sounds of it, for this to work, I was going to need to bleed. *A lot.*

"No, it's okay," I told him in as level a voice as I could. "Take the marrow. It works better, doesn't it?"

I could vaguely remember him saying something to that effect. Or maybe that he needed less of it than he did the blood to make it work.

Or some shit like that.

Ethan gave me a pained nod. "It does."

"Then take it. I can handle it."

His adams apple bobbed. "I'm not sure I can."

It took me a second to understand, but then I realized what he was trying to say. *He* couldn't take it.

Ethan didn't want to hurt me.

"Well, just get one of the doctors to do it, then."

Ethan shook his head. "They aren't here. Azrael released them just after he brought us here. He didn't need them anymore."

"He released them?" I asked, incredulous. "Just like that?"

He didn't turn them into blood slaves? Lobotomize them? Kill them?

He'd…kept his word?

I could hardly believe it. It didn't make kidnapping and compelling three people any less horrid, but he didn't kill them, and I felt a little bit of the ice wall I'd build against him soften and melt.

Ethan seemed confused. He raised his brows at me.

"Yeah. What else did you think he was going to do with them?"

I didn't like how Ethan asked me that question. Like he already trusted Azrael and he was confused as to why I didn't. Had he forgotten what Azrael did?

It seemed I wasn't the only one wondering because Frost came speeding into view, his face contorted in a scowl. "Don't be so quick to trust the bastard who almost got us killed. Or did you forget that I had to drag your ass out of the burning wreckage of Rose's truck?"

Ethan, unfazed, merely shrugged. "Things have changed, Cam."

I blinked, both at Ethan's nonchalance and his casual use of the nickname he *and only he* ever called Camden Frost. "Not that much," Frost warned. "We need to keep our guard up."

Frost's icy stare slid to me and I felt my face blanche. "That means you too, Rosie."

I bit down, pressing my teeth together to keep myself from barking out a scathing retort. Because Frost was right. I *was* letting my guard down. And if he saw it, then I was sure that meant they all did.

A furious blush found its way into my cheeks and I shouldered past Frost before he could see it. "I'll meet you in the lab," I called back to Ethan, wanting nothing more than to get as far as I could from Frost's questioning stare.

ETHAN MUST HAVE APOLOGIZED FOR HAVING TO TAKE MY blood and marrow about a dozen times before he finally let me leave the lab. The puncture marks from where his needled slid into my flesh and bone were already pretty much healed.

He'd been pale as he's extracted the fluids from my body, and by the look on his face, you'd think *he* was the one having a sharp metal bit rammed into his spine. Poor guy.

It was just after sundown and we were following Azrael outside. I realized, a little belatedly, that I'd never asked where we were. I assumed some place south, but it didn't seem to matter at the time.

Now, though, a crawling feeling of unease settled in my stomach. "Where are we?" I asked, posing the question to no one in particular as we ascended the front steps and followed Azrael through the garden opposite where we sat that morning, down a little flagstone pathway, and around the side of the house.

"Italy." It was Blake who answered, one dark brow arched back in my direction as though to say, *you really didn't know?*

My pulse picked up. "What?" I demanded, stopping on the path. "What the hell are we doing in fucking Italy?"

It had to be some sort of joke, right?

But the air between Blake and I was stagnant. He was *not* joking.

Azrael turned back from his spot at the head of the line and smirked. "I suppose I should have mentioned that."

"You think?"

My mind raced to catch up. "How did we even get here?"

"We flew," Frost offered. "On Azrael's *private jet.*"

My brows were dangerously close to getting lost in my hairline.

Fuck. I must have been really out of it.

"Amala was here. I knew we needed the skill of a healer and she's the only one I've ever convinced to work for me."

Hmmm, I wonder why...

Azrael sniggered at me. "She keeps this place warded against being discovered by other vampires, or other witches. It's the only place where no one can find us."

I opened my mouth to protest, but Azrael hushed me and waved me forward. "Before you lose your very fragile temper, dear Rose, why don't you come and see what I've got for you?"

What? With pursed lips and a sharp glare, I moved past Blake and Frost to stand by Azrael and looked to where he indicated at the edge of the path. Between the tall hedges and low bushes dotted with tiny pink flowers was something sleek and black, glinting in the moonlight.

I turned back to Az. "It's yours," he said, and gave me a little shove. "As promised."

It took me a moment to realize what the hell he was talking about, then my spine stiffened, and I stared at him incredulously. "You didn't."

"Oh," he said devilishly. "I did."

Tearing my gaze from his smug face, I raced to the

ELENA LAWSON

edge of the pathway and squealed. He actually fucking did.

He bought me a new truck.

A new fucking truck.

It was a newer model of my Betty. A bit larger, with all the bells and whistles I could never have afforded. He even added big round off-road lights mounted to the top of the cab on a shining silver bar.

"Ultraviolet," he explained. "In case you're ever in a jam."

I grinned.

Oh yes.

The thought of frying a bunch of vamps with my fancy headlights brought a smile of pure joy to my face.

Azrael shook his head at me, and I contained my daydreams of barbequed baddies and put my hand on my hips. "Well don't expect me to thank you," I said, inhaling sharply. "The way I see it, you *owed* me this truck. You owe me a lot more."

He didn't even try to argue, meeting my gaze with genuine gratitude of his own. "I do," he agreed.

Unsure how to respond to that I just nodded. "Good," I replied, stepping up to the driver's side door. "And I'll be needing you to get this baby back to the states for me when we go home."

Azrael's eyes narrowed in thought. "I'll just buy you another."

"No," I almost shouted, admiring the leather interior with teary-eyed reverence. "I want *her*," I told him. "She's perfect."

60

"Very well."

"What'll you name her?" Frost asked, barely able to conceal the obvious disdain in his voice.

I smoothed my hand over the supple leather of the seat and fingered the petal-soft dash, not a single spec of dust on it. I had half a mind to call her Betty after my dearly departed, but no truck could replace her.

This was a new beast and she deserved a new name.

I grinned.

"Petal," I decided, still reveling in the feel of her as I caught sight of the shining silver key ring and bulky fob in the ignition. I started her engine and she fucking *purred*.

"Petal?" Blake asked with a pinched face, taking in her sleek frame. "Really?"

Frost snorted. "A bit...*tame* isn't it?"

"They call me the Black *Rose*," I crooned triumphantly. "Would you call *me* tame, Camden Frost?"

He clamped his mouth shut.

"Didn't think so," I trilled, shutting my door and rolling down the window—*oh my fucking god even the windows worked!*

"Well, what are you waiting for?" I asked, revving Petal's engine. "Let's go get us some more vampires."

CHAPTER 6

urned out we were only a little over an hour south of Naples. The drive was *glorious.* Petal was a fucking beast of a truck. She didn't protest as we made our way out over uneven gravel roads, and then she lengthened her strides once we hit the blacktop. Her cadence so steady we could have been flying instead of chewing pavement.

We hadn't found any in the two small villages we passed along the way, but that didn't surprise me. Vamps tended to hang out in larger centers. It was easier to blend in when there were hundreds of thousands of other faces. People going missing or turning up dead or without memory were more easily swept under rugs and forgotten.

I felt the presence of vampiric energy almost immediately after we entered the city. The energy in the truck was enough to choke me already, what with Frost, Blake, and Azrael sharing the cab… but I was starting to recognize their own particular *flavor* of energy.

And this was different. *Other.*

My hands tightened on Petal's slick black steering wheel as I pulled into a parking lot next to a mostly vacant plaza. "This place must be crawling with them," I muttered as I shut off the engine and stepped outside to get a better feel of the place and some fresh air.

Azrael pursed his lips as he came around the truck. "It's near to where we first landed after leaving Emeris. This is the original birthplace of the Vocari people on mortal soil."

I nodded. "Great."

Frost and Blake didn't seem to like that bit of information but said nothing.

"Guess we should get to work," I said with a sigh and adjusted the strap of my katana, double checked my stakes were in place, my daggers were sheathed in my boots, and the long sterling silver chopsticks were still securing my hair in a tight black bun at the top of my head.

"How are we going to do this?" Blake asked, shrugging out of his light jacket to leave it in the truck.

I looked to Azrael, but he offered no insight.

Okay then…

"Well, we need an army," I began, getting momentarily distracted by the scent of salted pasta on the breeze. *Fuuuuuck.* I promised myself that once we were finished, I'd make Azrael buy me some before we went back to his mansion in the hills. As much as I loved Estelle's cooking, I doubted it could compare to fresh Italian pasta.

"Rose?" Frost hedged.

"Right," I continued, giving my head a little shake to clear it. "Um, so we need an army, but we also know that Raphael is still trying to build his own army. Basically, it's us or him."

Blake cocked his head. "I'm not following."

"What she's saying is we give any vampires we find a choice: join us or die," Azrael answered for me and we shared a look that made my skin crawl.

"Are you serious?" Blake hissed, his expression giving away his shock. "That's it? Just choose a side or die?"

I winced, trying to think of a path that wouldn't lead to my guys thinking I was some sort of deranged monster just as bad as Raphael. Thinking of Frost, Ethan, and Blake helped. They didn't kill for sport. They did their best to live their lives peacefully as the monsters they chose to become.

There could be others like them. And if there were, would I force them to choose or die?

I sucked in a breath. "Okay. You're right. We can't just kill all the ones who won't join…" *even though I wouldn't be entirely opposed to the idea,* I finished in my own mind and noticed Azrael lifting a brow in my direction. He didn't comment, though, and I was grateful.

"We use Az," I said, pointing to the mass of muscle across from me in the lot. "He can read minds."

Frost squinted. "And how are we going to use that to our advantage here?"

"He'll tell us their intentions. We can give any we find

the choice to join us and have a taste of the sun or stay out of the fight entirely."

"And if they don't," Azrael continued, picking up on my train of thought. "If they state that they are with my brother—or deny it but have opposing thoughts," he trailed off.

"*Then* we'll kill them," I said cheerfully. "That work for you two?"

They both nodded and I was reminded once more how they used to kill the bad vamps, too. This wasn't so different, was it? We couldn't let any of the vamps who had allegiances to Raphael go free. If we did, we would only be ensuring an even bigger fight later.

I was sure they understood that.

"Great," I said while clapping my hands together and rubbing them. I let the little bristle of excitement running over my skin grow to a full-on shiver. The adrenaline boost kicked my body into a higher gear, and I grinned. "Let's start over there," I told them, pointing to a cluster of run-down buildings at the end of the next block. I could feel the pulse of their otherworldly energy coming from that direction.

I'd be able to home in on it better once we got closer.

"Can you tell how many?" I asked Azrael as we began to walk out of the lot and down the mostly quiet street.

A few passersby caught sight of me between the three walls of muscle walking around me in a spearhead formation and hurried a little faster to their destinations.

Azrael clucked his tongue and tipped his head to one side, cracking his neck as he listened to the distant sounds and the inner voices of the vamps. "About ten. Maybe a few more than that."

My eyes widened. It was a good-sized nest. "They have a queen?"

He nodded. "They're pleasuring her at the moment."

I stopped. "Maybe we should wait."

Azrael paused and spun to give me a questioning stare. He shook his head when I refused to move, his eyes rolling to the heavens.

Frost snorted and Blake pulled his bottom lip between his teeth, chuckling low in his throat.

I may have been a murderous bitch, but I wasn't a complete monster. I shrugged. "What? If we're going to end up killing them all, we can at least let her climax first. I'm not *that* mean."

Five vampires.

Fucking *five*. After approaching three vampire nests that was all we had to show for ourselves. I supposed it was better than a big fat fucking zero, but it was a lot less than I'd been hoping for, especially since we'd been out most of the night and would have to be heading back to the house soon.

The windows in the truck were coated with UV blocking heavy tint, so as long as I got the guys back into the truck before sunup, we could keep hunting for a little longer.

"It's somewhere here," I muttered, bitter, and hungry, and getting tired.

I hadn't even been able to kill anything yet.

I itched to use my stakes.

My katana was screaming with the urge to behead skulls from spines.

But most of all…I was fucking *bored.*

"It's above us," said Azrael, gesturing to the dirt streaked roof. The building was abandoned—an old office building maybe, three floors with a warehouse on the bottom floor where we entered. It was filled with old rusted metal barrels and frayed extension cords. The ceiling tiles were stained with water marks and the exterior was in disrepair.

"Above us?"

The stairway leading up was blocked. Completely covered over in debris to purposefully stop anyone from trying to go upstairs. Desks, chairs, cushions, even massive piles of paper and books crowded the stairs all the way up as far as we could see from this angle.

There had to be another way up.

I scanned the ceiling, smirking when I found the lip of warped tile where there was clearly a bloody handprint. Moving beneath it, I glanced into the darkened slit and saw a sliver of light.

They tunneled through the second floor, I thought purposefully toward Azrael.

I pointed without speaking. They had to know we were there. It was too early for them all to already be asleep, and even if they were, not everyone was as heavy of a sleeper as I was.

Azrael took the lead as he had when we'd found the

other three nests, reaching up to tear the tile away. The air above was dark now, proving my theory correct.

They'd just extinguished the lights.

I peered up into the dark hole and the metallic smell of fresh blood fell over us like mist, wrinkling my nose.

Fuck.

It was fresh.

Either they'd just opened a fuckload of blood bags or there was a mortal up there somewhere—bleeding out.

I drew my stakes, my fingers curling around the metal warmed from the heat of my thighs.

Maybe we should have brought the others, I thought, but shook my head. The five vampires we'd managed to convince to join us were weak. It was clear from when we first spotted them that they hadn't fed in at least a few days, if not longer. Besides, we'd left them near the truck in case they had to pile into the back beneath the roll-top cover.

We'd told them we'd return before sunrise, but I'd unlocked it for them just in case. I didn't like the idea of leaving them with my brand new baby, but Azrael had compelled them to remain there, and only to get into the truck if or when the sun rose.

"They wouldn't have been any use to us in their condition," Azrael whispered, a lick of distaste staining his features. He was clearly just as disappointed in our current vampire haul as I was. At this rate, we wouldn't have enough vamps to fill out a sports team, let alone a fucking army.

Patience, I reminded myself, rolling my shoulders back. *Rome wasn't built in a day.*

I smirked at the reference, wondering offhandedly how far Naples was away from Rome.

"You've never been?" Azrael asked as Blake and Frost moved to where Az and I were standing peering up into the vampire hidey hole.

"To Rome? No. I've never even been anywhere in Europe."

His brows pulled together and something tender passed over his face, making my jaw clench as I tore my gaze from him.

Azrael was quiet for another minute, long enough for Frost to shuffle impatiently from foot to foot and for me to start feeling a bit uncomfortable, before he hopped up into the dark and called back that it was clear in a barely audible whisper of breath.

Snapping myself out of the strange feeling spreading through my chest, I inhaled sharply and jumped up, my fingers just catching the lip of the beam well enough to pull my body up into the ceiling and then the rest of the way up through the bored hole in the flooring and onto the second floor.

The telltale thuds of Frost and Blake followed right on my heels.

We followed Azrael through a dank corridor. The air was stale and fetid, but with a hint of something sweet and smoky. Like vanilla crème brûlée with too much burned sugar.

Like someone was burning something to purposely rid the space of the odors permeating it.

I could barely see as we moved through the maze of abandoned hallways, the floors littered with discarded data reports and tiny metal paperclips.

We were getting close now. I could feel the presence of them, and not just from one direction, but surrounding us.

I'd be bothered by that if not for the fact that Azrael was with us. There couldn't have been more than eight or nine of them in the nest. Azrael wouldn't have let me go in with him if there were more than he could handle.

We came upon a central part of the old office space. A hub where there were several low desks and carpeted pathways that lead down in five different directions. The rest of the space was open, and it was where I imagined a past team of data analysists would have once met over morning coffee with their team leads to go over numbers and graphs I'd never cared to understand.

Now, though, it was filled with the scent of death and decay.

Musty carpets and office furniture would have been bad enough, but the distinct odors of human decay and the tang of fresh blood added an extra layer of *ick*.

"Come out, come out, wherever you are," I called in a sing song voice, earning myself a scolding look from Frost. "We just want to talk."

I flipped the stakes around and around in my hands, amping myself up for the fight I wanted so fucking badly

71

to have. There was something really fucked up with my head, I knew that. Killing shit shouldn't make me giddy with childlike enthusiasm. But this wasn't killing—not really. Not to me, anyway.

This was putting corpses where they belonged: to rest.

Azrael was staring contemplative at me and I groaned. "Would you stop looking at me like that?" I snapped at him.

I'd been getting used to his rooting around in my mind at all hours of the day and night, but he didn't have any right to judge me for my *private* thoughts.

Azrael turned away as they began to approach. Two in each of the five hallways, including the hallway we'd just come down.

There was enough ambient light to see by, though I couldn't really tell where it was coming from.

I heard one of them whisper something and thought I caught the word *Raphael* in the hushed sentence. My body coiled, readying to strike, but Azrael set a slow, heavy hand on my shoulder, calming my urge for blood.

"I am *not* Raphael," Azrael said, releasing me to spin in a measured half circle, wide enough to meet each of their gazes.

"Azrael?" A woman asked, coming forward from the shadows to reveal a heart-shaped face framed in a mass of dark curling waves. Her dark eyes squinted at him. She was beautiful in the way that a king cobra is beautiful right before it bites you.

I didn't like her.

Azrael responded to the woman in Italian, and I craned my neck to look up at him. I shouldn't have been surprised, and I wasn't; not that he knew how to speak Italian, anyway...more because of how he sounded while doing it.

Holy fucking shit.

His voice curling around those foreign words made my toes curl and I couldn't help my mouth falling open as I listened to them banter back and forth.

I only managed to reign myself in when I noticed the vampires were starting to close in around us and their buzzing conversation with Azrael was growing more heated by the moment.

An itching sensation crawled up the back of my neck and I realized that more of them were arriving back to the nest. Rushing to return home after their feedings before sunrise.

I counted fourteen now.

No, eighteen.

Azrael, I thought loudly, his name rebounding in my skull. *At this rate we can still take them, but...*

I didn't finish the thought. Didn't have to.

If more came, there was no guarantee.

I had little doubt that Azrael could take them on alone, but not while also watching over my guys—which I *fully* expected him to do.

He couldn't keep them off himself *and* off them. He was ancient and therefore stronger and faster than any other vampire on earth, but he wasn't superman.

"Andiamo via adesso," said Azrael, his voice a venomous roar. "Se attacchi, *morirai*."

I wasn't an expert on Italian or anything, but I got the distinct feeling that he was threatening them. I just prayed they were smart enough to know when they were beat. There would be no victory for them here.

The female hissed, backed by three burly males who looked like they were jacked on steroids. "Partire!" she shouted at us, baring her fangs.

My throat went dry, and I held my breath, waiting for an attack, but it didn't come.

I was almost disappointed when Azrael curled his hand around the spot just above my elbow and pulled me back the way we came with Frost and Ethan following.

"What did she say?" I whispered harshly, resisting the urge to strike out at the smug vampires behind us as they moved out of the way to let us pass.

"Not yet," Azrael grunted. "Wait until we're outside."

"But—"

"*Rose.*"

I tugged my arm from his grip and kicked down the nearest office door. It burst from its hinges and clattered against the wall as I strode through and took three running steps before breaking through the reinforced glass window, stakes out.

I landed amidst a scattering of broken glass, a hand out to steady myself. The balls of my feet burned, but I didn't care.

Azrael, Frost, and Ethan were only a second behind me.

"The hell was that Rose?" Blake growled, wrenching me up from my crouch.

I ignored him, turning to Azrael. *"There,"* I said, spreading my hands wide at my sides. "Now we're outside. Explain."

"You're bleeding," Frost said tightly, and looked up to the busted glass window on the second floor. I followed his gaze and saw two vampires staring down at us from the landing. Both of them had fangs bared and looked like they were deciding whether it was worth it to attack.

Fucking bring it bitches...

But the one on the left pulled the taller one back, tilting his chin toward the horizon. I hadn't even noticed, but now that I saw them backing away, I realized how close to sunrise it was. We had maybe ten minutes before the first rays of dawn flashed over the edge of the world and reduced my guys to cinders.

"They won't join us," Azrael said without further explanation, following my line of sight to the brightening sky with a tight jaw.

"I gathered that," I retorted, sheathing my stakes. I guess I wasn't going to quench their thirst tonight. "Run ahead back to the truck," I told them, sweeping the loose hairs away from my face and back into the bun on my head. "We're cutting it too close."

"I'll carry you," Frost offered, but I stepped away as he reached out for me.

"No."

"No?"

75

"They're with Raphael, aren't they?" I asked, turning to face Azrael in the pale light of the approaching dawn.

He licked his lips. "They are."

"Then they need to be dealt with."

No one said anything.

"If we don't deal with them now, we'll just have to deal with them later, when they have rallied *more* vampires to Raphael's cause."

You know I'm right, I added for Azrael's benefit.

"There isn't time," he replied aloud.

"I don't need you," I said monotone, standing resolute as I looked up at the building. "Go. Bring the truck here. I'll be waiting."

I let Azrael read my thoughts. He wouldn't leave unless he knew my plan. His eyes widened, but barely enough that you would notice if you weren't looking for such a change. Then his expression hardened. "I can't risk losing you," he said in a low timbre.

"You won't."

"What the hell are you talking about?" Blake demanded, clearly getting antsy at the approach of the sun.

"Let me do this," I appealed to Azrael. "If you hurry, you'll be back here in ten minutes and I'll already be done."

Finally, Azrael nodded, and I smiled.

"Let's go," Azrael said.

"Not a fucking chance," Frost said, his face reddening. He crossed his arms, glaring at me. "The fuck you think you're doing Rosie?"

I shook my head. "Chill out tough guy. I'll be fine. I promise. I just need a few minutes to take out the trash, and you guys need to get your asses out of the sun."

"What are you going—"

I grabbed Frost by the shoulder and pulled him down to my level, whispering harshly in his ear. I didn't want to say it aloud for risk of them hearing me inside the building, but stubborn ass really wasn't going to leave until he knew exactly what the fuck was going on. "I'm going to burn it to the ground," I hissed. "And I'm going to stand out here, *in the sun,* and watch the bonfire, *okay?*"

He reeled back as though stung, looking down at me through slitted eyes.

"Satisfied?"

He gulped and nodded to Blake to tell him that it was alright to leave me.

They turned to walk away and I followed them as though I were leaving with them, making a good show of keeping pace with them until we were out of sight, then I broke off from the line and winked at Blake when he tossed me a panicked look over his shoulder.

I mouthed the words *see you soon* and took off down a side alleyway where we'd passed a tiny shop half a block away on the corner earlier that night. It was a closet of a store, with clustered shelves and bagged chips hanging from the ceiling, but it was the only thing I'd seen open anywhere nearby at this time of morning.

The bell chimed as I stepped inside and made straight for the counter where a young man was sitting with a bag of chips open on his lap and his phone open to a video player showing flashes of naked skin. The unmistakable sound of a woman's acted moans as she pretended to enjoy the mediocre fucking she was being given told me *exactly* was he was doing to pass his time.

"Hey little shit," I said, leaning over the counter so that my breasts were pushed up and in full view. "These are a lot nicer than those. Want to see?"

He stood, trying to hide an erection and greeted me in Italian. Oh, right. How was this going to work in another language?

His eyes met mine and I let the power of my compulsion flood through the connection. His face went slack and I pointed to the tray of lighters behind the counter. "Lighter," I commanded.

He cocked his head at me.

"Torch," I tried again.

Nope nada.

"Fire."

His glazed eyes fell on the lighters and he lifted a black one from the tray and procured a bottle of lighter fluid from beneath the counter before placing both into my waiting hands. I grinned.

"Fire," he repeated back to be almost robotically, his accent butchering the word.

"Thanks, sweety. You can go back to your video now."

He blinked and lifted his phone to his face. "Video..." he murmured and wandered absently back to his chair and slumped down into it, pressing play again.

Oh well, I thought and turned to leave the shop, letting

the door bang closed behind me. *He'll snap out of it in a minute.*

I skipped back toward the building just as the sun crested the horizon, painting the tops of the white-washed buildings in hues of gold and fiery orange. Once I was satisfied that the sun was high enough that there were little to no shadows a vampire could hide within, I began to whistle as I skipped.

An old man exiting his building in a threadbare robe with a wooden pipe hanging from his thick lower lip paused in his tracks, taking in the sight of me instead of the rising sun. He bent backward to crack his back and fumbled to catch his pipe as it fell from his mouth, scattering hot tobacco coals over the crack sidewalk.

He shouted something after me in Italian, but the blood rushing in my ears and thrum of the hunt in my chest blocked out the indecipherable words.

The city was waking, and even though this area of it was less inhabited than the central core—mostly made up of older buildings and warehouses—there would be too many people to compel if they saw. I had to be quick.

Racing the last half a block, I was left standing in a swath of warm sunlight at the building's front. I stepped up to the exterior wall and kicked in a ground-level window. The glass shattered, filling the first floor we'd entered onto earlier. Twisting the cap off the little white bottle, I squeezed the lighter fluid into the space, twisting it in my grip to spell out the words ROSE WAS HERE in a pretty cursive on the dirty-strewn floor with a straight line leading up to where I was. A liquid fuse.

I grinned at my handiwork and reached into my pocket for the slim black lighter.

A small whimper echoed from above, and I wondered if they could smell the fluid and knew what was coming for them already.

But then the whimper turned to a cry of anguish and my fingers stilled on the lighter. I leaned in and inhaled deeply, trying to smell past the stench of lighter fluid and must to find what I was looking for—what I *hoped* I wouldn't find.

The smell of fresh blood was still there. Still *fresh*.

There had been no sign that they had a live human in there with them earlier, though, I was sure of it.

I ground my teeth, my heart suddenly in my throat.

The whimper came again, and I cursed myself, knowing I was about to do exactly what I promised the guys I wouldn't. If there was a human still alive in there, I had to try to save them.

What if it's a trap?

It might be.

What if they're waiting for you to come back inside?

That's possible.

While I was having a little internal argument with myself, the small cries of the human woman became softer and I wondered if she was even going to make it if I saved her. Or had they drained her to the point of death, already?

I sighed heavily and felt all my muscles tense. This was what I'd wanted, wasn't it? I bit my lower lip and curled my fingernails into my palms, grounding myself with the shock of the pain.

I drew my stakes and peered inside the shadow of the building. Without the dirty window in the way, the sunlight filled the lower level with its golden glow. Catching my breath, I slunk inside, following the path of the sun's glow, staying in its warmth just in case.

I climbed down onto a filing cabinet and then down further onto the floor, careful not to step in the lighter fluid. Barely breathing, I crept to the base of the opening that led to the second floor and squinted up into the dark. The cries of the girl were so faint I had to strain to hear them, but they were still there.

She was up there, a little ways down the hall to my right if my ears didn't lie. An idea sparked in my mind and I clambered back out the busted window and cupped my hands over my eyes to look up at the second floor, where the guys and I had jumped out of the window. It was to the right of the hole on the lower level. She had to be near that office. Probably right next door to it.

I winced as I heard the rumbling purr of an engine coming up the street behind me. I didn't dare look. The feeling of Azrael's approach was a hair-raising itch on the back of my neck. They were here, and they weren't going to like what they saw.

Sorry guys...

Pulling myself up the outside exterior of the building, I climbed from tiny ledge to tiny ledge, using my fingertips and the edges of my rubber-soled boots to get the traction I needed.

Once I was close enough, I used all my upper body strength to pull myself into the second story room, careful not to disturb the piles of broken glass on the carpet. They may have heard me bust the window down-stairs, but I made sure they wouldn't hear me climb up here.

Let them think I was downstairs. I only needed a minute to get her out. One minute and then I'd be back outside in the safety of the sun.

I heard the engine rev downstairs. It was a warning. They were trying to call me back out without lowering the windows or honking the horn.

Steadying myself with a breath, I trusted in the sun on my back. As long as I was inside this room, they couldn't come for me. And if my plan worked, I wouldn't have to leave this room to get what I wanted.

I pressed my ear up against the wall on the left, closing my eyes to focus all my energy on listening to what was happening on the other side. It took so long I was starting to wonder if I'd been wrong, but then, after a few minutes, it was there; the pained whimper of a girl. Unmistakable.

It was all the proof I needed. Sheathing my stakes, I reached up and pulled the katana from its holster, shiv-ering at the sound the sharp metal blade made as it exited its scabbard. Fuck, I loved that sound.

Two steps back, swing hard.

The blade sliced through the drywall like butter.

Swing again.

An 'X' was formed in the wall.

A swinging kick and the wall busted inwards,

revealing a girl no more than eighteen, with sun-stained brown hair matted down with dried and wet blood. A vampire hissed as the entrails of sunlight poured into his lair, jarring him enough that he released her thigh from his mouth and retracted his fingers from where they were doing some horrible thing beneath her skirt.

My temper flared red hot. My vision blurred with the crimson tinge of bloodlust. He was *mine.*

I stepped in and wrenched the girl out of the way, maybe too roughly, but I got her away from the blood-sucking motherfucker who had her. I figured I had maybe three more seconds before the rest of the nest spilled into the room.

Good thing I only needed two.

One for his balls.

And another for his head.

I had him castrated in less than a second. It was easily done since the muscled bastard was completely naked. His cock erect. I shuddered to think what he would have done if I hadn't stopped him.

The millisecond of horror in his eyes and the wide 'O' of his mouth as he stared down at his severed cock and balls on the carpet gave me the satisfaction, I wanted a fraction of a second before I took his head. The heavy chunk of useless flesh toppled to the floor, his mouth still open wide and his eyes still staring in horror as they came level with his severed bits and pieces.

I stepped backward into the light just as the door burst open and the queen of the nest stepped inside, flanked by the three muscled bloodsuckers from earlier.

I bowed low, scooping up the half-conscious girl as I continued backing into the sun. The girl under one arm and my blood-stained katana in the other.

"*Sei morto*," the vampire woman hissed, her black eyes narrowing.

I cocked my head at her. Understanding that *morto* meant something to do with death, so I was pretty sure she just threatened me.

Pouting, I tilted my head back at her. "No," I said. "I'm afraid you're the one who's about to die."

Without another word save for a hastily called *toodooloo!* and a smile, I jumped back down onto the street and waved to the truck that was still idling on the roadside.

"I'll just be a second," I called to them, unable to see through the extreme tint of the windows, but I knew they could hear me. "Picked up a stray!"

I pointed to the limp body as I set her gingerly down to rest against the ground. I sheathed my katana and switched it for the lighter, leaning into the window to find the end of my lighter fluid trail.

Ah.

There it is.

It took a couple tries since my hands were sticky with blood. The low murmur of voice upstairs was turning into full on shouting as the vampire nest within realized what was about to happen to them.

Once upon a time I felt something when I killed them.

But not anymore.

And especially not after seeing what they were about to let happen to an innocent girl.

Fuck no.

If anything, I wanted to dance around the building while it burned. But there wasn't time for that, either.

The girl needed a healer if she was going to survive, and I happened to know a witch who was supposedly the best. *If* Azrael would allow me to bring her with us.

"There we go," I said as the trail lit in a *whoosh* of fire and spread down into the room, the flames consuming papers and spreading fast through the bottom floor. "Welcome to hell, bitches!" I called up toward them, loud enough so they would all hear me, not caring that they probably couldn't understand.

The screech of a dying vamp filled the morning air as I lifted the girl from the ground and carried her to the truck. They'd positioned Petal so the sun rising to the east would leave one side of the truck in shadow, allowing me to open the door without scalding them inside.

I opened the back door and found Blake sitting next to Azrael. Frost was in the driver's seat up front.

The second it opened, Blake grabbed hold of the girl and pulled her onto his lap but the whole time he was glaring at me. "You're a fucking idiot," he hissed, his eyes flashing with a dangerous glint.

The girl whimpered again, and I set my sights on Azrael. "We're bringing her back with us. She needs a healer."

"I don't—"

"We're bringing her with us," I demanded, leaving no

room for argument in my voice this time. Judging by the way she jerked when I wrapped my arm around her middle, I had to guess she had at least a few broken ribs. And her ankle was clearly broken, too, her foot twisted at an odd angle. Those injuries combined with her massive blood loss would make it difficult for a regular hospital to save her. And even if they could, it would take her months to fully heal.

We could heal her in days so long as Amala would help us.

Azrael's jaw clenched, but he didn't argue any further.

"Get. In." Frost's voice came sharply from the front seat.

Uh-oh.

I closed the back door and opened the front, chewing my lower lip as I looked up at Frost. "I'm...sorry?" I tried shrinking back from his coiled body.

I wasn't actually sorry, and I think he knew that, but it was worth a shot.

He released his death grip on the steering wheel and scooted over to the empty passenger seat, letting me get in. I closed the door behind me and gulped, feeling the tension like a thick fog in the cab of the truck.

"I couldn't just leave her there," I muttered to Frost. "You wouldn't have left her there, either. Admit it."

He crossed his arms over his chest and stewed.

I sighed and glanced back at the building that was now almost entirely engulfed in flames. It really was a beautiful sight.

"You're..." Frost began in a low growl, still not looking

at me, but he trailed off as though he couldn't even begin to find the right word to use in this situation.

"Magnificent," Azrael finished for him. "She's magnificent."

"I was going to say something more like stupid and reckless," Frost said, his voice evening out as he finally turned his attention onto me, his bright green eyes boring holes into my soul. His nostrils flared. "But yes. She is that, too."

CHAPTER 7

From the tension in the truck, I knew it was probably best not to speak, and I managed pretty well with the radio turned to a low hum, at least until we got back to the house and pulled into a large parking garage around back.

Azrael passed the injured girl to Frost to bring inside, and that was when Azrael turned on me.

"You will never be that reckless again," he told me, and for a second I was afraid he'd compelled me but didn't feel the usual strain associated with his compulsion. It was an order, not a forced command.

My face heated. "You *knew* she was in there," I accused him and felt my stomach drop when he didn't deny it. I was fishing, I hadn't known for certain until just now.

But of course, he knew. He was reading all of their thoughts. He'd have heard hers somewhere in that building, too. He'd have heard her heart beating.

"I did," he replied after a minute, his voice monotone

89

as he looked down the bridge of his nose at me. "It was not our business."

"Not our... *are you fucking kidding me?* You would have just left her to *die* in there? To be fucking raped and bled dry?"

His expression hardened. "There are terrible things happening all over the world right now, Rose. This very instant. You can't stop every bad thing from happening. If I'd demanded the release of their meal, they would have atta—"

"Their *meal?*"

"Rose," Blake warned.

Frost had hesitated by the thick metal door that I assumed led into the house. His square jaw clenched as though he was praying for an excuse to attack Azrael. And *I* was the idiot.

"If I *ever* have the chance to save a mortal life from *your* kind," I hissed, jabbing a sharp fingernail into his buff chest. "I will take it."

His brows lifted and he exhaled through his nose. He turned to Frost with eyes glittering with fury. "I see what you mean now," he said in a gruff voice. "She's incorrigible."

A faint knocking came from the back of the truck and I jumped, having all but forgotten about the five vampires we'd wrangled in Naples. Azrael tore himself away from me and went around to pop the release, letting the sardined vamps out from the bed of Petal.

They gasped as they came out, as though they'd been unable to breathe for the whole drive. *Oops.*

One scented the bleeding human and hissed, backing away, I assumed to try to keep himself from attacking. "Don't even think about it," I warned the bone-thin vamp. "There are blood bags inside. You can wait."

His chest stopped moving, and the others followed suit, holding their breath.

"Rose," Blake said again, this time more frantic as he raced to the girl in Frost's arms. "Shit, her heart is failing."

I dropped my hand from pointing at the ragtag group of vamps and rushed to corral Frost inside. "Go!" I shouted at him. "Someone go find Amala."

Frost muscled his way into the house, and Blake vanished in a flash of black hair and pale muscle down the hall to find the witch.

Ethan appeared out from the makeshift lab as we barreled down toward the front of the house. His eyes widened on the blood-drained girl in Frost's arms. "What —" he stammered. "Who is that?"

"A human," I said, breathless as I pushed past him into the lab and cleared some papers and an empty beaker off the couch. "Put her down."

Frost set her gently against the gilt patterned cushions, and her head lolled to one side. "Hey," I said, slapping her cheek gently. She didn't respond.

"I need you to stay awake," I all but shouted into her face.

This was someone's daughter.

Or someone's best friend.

Maybe someone's girlfriend.

Judging by her outfit. A short skirt and pretty purple top, she'd been out on a date—or maybe dancing.

Her only mistake was probably taking a wrong turn onto a street a little too close to the vampire nest. But it was also possible they'd hunted her at a club and compelled her to go with them. I'd killed a few with that same MO.

Heat pooled in my stomach like acid and I pushed her hair from her face, leaning down to listen for breath at her red lipstick stained mouth. There was nothing.

"She isn't breathing," I said, feeling my body begin to shake.

Dead vamps I could deal with, but this...

I couldn't ever stand finding the dead humans in their nests. It didn't happen very often. They were smart about disposing of the evidence. And many fed and then compelled their victims to forget before sending them on their way.

"Rose," Azrael's voice was soft as he kneeled beside me on the rug.

I plugged the girl's nose and blew into her mouth, tasting the acrid flavors of blood and stale vodka on my tongue. Then I began chest compressions, counting in my head, left wondering if I was doing it too fast, or too slow. How many compressions was it? Was I pressing to hard? Her ribs were broken, I didn't want to break more of them.

"Rose," this time it was Ethan. "She's gone."

I blew into her mouth again and shuddered, my stomach roiling as a vivid image of my mother, drenched in her own blood flashed before my eyes. I didn't stop. Thirty compressions. Two breaths. Thirty compressions. Two breaths.

I remembered her face. Pale and slack jawed. Her eyes dull and lifeless. I remembered the sound of my own scream, foreign to my ears just before he sliced my throat and left me for dead, clawing toward my mom, trying despite bleeding out myself, to try and save her.

For a terrifying second when my eyes flew open, I saw her there on the couch instead of the girl in the purple shirt. My mom, broken and bleeding. I cried out and jumped back from the girl, shaking all over.

Strong hands came around my shoulders and I flinched. In a knee-jerk reaction I had a stake unholstered, raised, and ready to strike, but Ethan caught the sharp end of the steel before I could pierce his flesh.

Coming back to myself, I dropped the stake and fell against him just as Amala and Blake crashed into the lab, knocking over a set of liquid-filled jars on a table near the door.

"It's okay," Ethan said in a hushed tone, whispering the words into the top of my head as he held me. One arm around my middle and the other cupping the back of my skull.

"Someone get her a drink," I heard him rasp. "Something with some sugar in it."

I heard Frost's heavy, clomping footsteps as he left the room.

I was shaking my head against Ethan's soft shirt, trying to wrap my head about what just happened. I hadn't known her. She was just another human. One of many to die by vampire hands. But I was so certain bringing her back here was the right move. I thought we were going to save her.

That *I* was going to save her.

That she was going to get to go home and not remember a thing of the terrible night she'd been victim to.

Now she wasn't going anywhere.

I didn't know why it was hitting me so hard, but I couldn't shake the feeling that I'd made a mistake. I should have brought her to a human hospital. She would have spent months healing, yes. But she might have lived if they could've gotten her a blood transfusion fast enough.

"Death took her swiftly," Azrael said quietly from where he was still knelt next to the girl. He reached up and shut her eyes. "She was weak, but her heart still beat strong in the truck. It must have been moving her that did it. It's not your fault."

"Fuck you," I croaked against Ethan.

"If it will make you any less upset, she will live again."

Oh shit.

I completely forgot.

I turned out of Ethan's arms and stared at her in a new light. She was dead, yes. But she wasn't gone. She'd been fed on. Multiple times.

Her blood was tainted with vampire venom. She *died* with vampire venom in her system and she wasn't fully drained of blood, only mostly.

She would come back.

I moved back to her on the couch and bent over her face, pushing her eyelids open. The bloodshot veins around her lifeless iris' were already receding. She was already beginning the transition.

"Fuck."

In trying to save her, had I just condemned her to an immortal life as a vampire?

"God fucking damnit!"

A thin gold chain around her neck glinted in the light, and I saw a name etched in gold cursive on the necklace. *Valentina.*

Taking a steadying breath, I rose. "Her name is Valentina," I said to no one in particular. She looked to be no more than nineteen. Maybe twenty. I peeled my gaze away from her, unable to look at what I'd done for another second. "Someone reset her ankle and get her cleaned up before she wakes. I don't want the first thing she feels to be pain."

And I didn't want her to look in the mirror when she awoke to see the evidence of the horrors inflicted on her. I didn't want her first immortal memory to be her own face in the state that it was in.

Without another word, I walked from the room and went upstairs, numbly undressing as I made my way toward the promise of a hot shower.

CHAPTER 8

*T*he water eased some of the tension out of my body and uncoiled my still muscles. The numbness seeped out of my bones first, and then slowly, my mind followed, and I sighed, leaning against the shower wall for support.

A burst of cold hit my back and I whirled around to find a naked Frost standing in the shower door, obscured by a wall of shifting steam. "Can I join you?" he asked gruffly, and I shuffled backwards to allow him space to enter. The shower was large, more like a small room than a shower stall, with walls tiled all the way around in a warm brown with threads of orange and gold. A seat was built into the furthest recess of it, with a rain head shower that I didn't currently have turned on over top of it. It was dim and filled with the blurring warmth of steam. But with Frost inside, it seemed so much smaller, his massive frame taking up more than half of the available space.

I shifted out of the stream of water so he could step

into it, and turned on the rain head, leaning against the seat to give him room.

He dipped his head into the warm cascade and sighed, brushing blood-coated hands over it as he moved out of the water and pushed the silvery strands of his hair out of his eyes.

He peered down at me, catching me studying the curve of his body under the deluge of hot water. The bulge of his perfect glutes. The cut of his muscled thighs and calves. The rippled muscle of his abs tapered down into the narrow Adonis belt of his waist.

"I'm sorry," he said, his eyes drooping down at the corners as he watched me through the thick fog.

I cocked my head at him, raising a brow. Frost never apologized. Like...*never.* He was like me in that regard. We were bad at the emotional stuff. Or at least, we were bad at talking about it. Saying words like *I'm sorry* or *I love you* didn't come easy to us like it did for others.

So, I let his apology sink in, knowing how hard it was for him to say, and that the fact he went to the trouble to say it meant that he wanted me to know how much he meant it.

"You were right," he rasped, wiping a wide paw over his mouth to brush stray droplets of water away. "I would have gone back for her, too."

I already knew that, but I nodded anyway, giving him the white flag, he was after. Truth be told, I'd forgiven the brute pretty much right after he was done being pissy.

"I just..." he said, his voice strained and uneven. "I can't stand the thought of you in danger and I *hated* not being able to go to you. To help you," his tone tipped upward into a growl near the end, his frustration showing through.

"I know," I said in a small voice, wanting to reassure him, but unable to. There was nothing I could do to fix that except to keep doing what I was doing. Keep giving blood to Ethan to make time-sensitive vamp sunblock, and to hopefully *one day* find a cure for vampirism. But that seemed *very* unlikely.

Frost reached out and pulled me to him from the seat until my breasts pressed against his ribs, our skin sliding together from the slipperiness of the water. "You know me," he said, his eyes piercing. "I-I have a problem with not being in control."

I set my hands against his chest and peered up at him, my body coming alive from his rough touch. "I know that, too."

He was always overprotective. Always trying to control the situation. Control *us* when he thought we needed to be controlled. But he was working on it, and that was really all I could ask.

"I—" his voice broke and he snapped his jaw shut. He didn't have to say it. I could see it there in his eyes. The torture. The pain. The wanting.

All the horrible, beautiful emotions that love evoked from you all at once. It hurt and it healed. It broke and it mended.

I knew because I felt it, too. The broken pieces of us finding where they fit with each other. Soon, we would be whole.

"Me, too," I whispered, and he dipped his head down to brush his warm lips against mine. The kiss was soft and so unlike him. It undid me in ways I didn't even know I could be undone. My belly dropped to my toes and my fingers curled around him, pulling him closer to me.

A tiny sound escaped me as his thick arms came around me, holding me flush against him. The warm water trickled over our heads and down the hollow between my breasts, tantalizing.

The kiss changed, became more fevered as I reached a hand down between us and stroked the length of his cock. He groaned against my mouth and I tugged his bottom lip in between my teeth, biting on it playfully to elicit another groan from his chest.

His cock became hard in my hand within seconds, and I luxuriated in the feel of the silk covered steel, all slippery and wet. Frost moved his hands to grip me by the shoulders, lifting me from the floor. I let loose a little yelp as he set me down on the tall tiled seat beneath the rain-head at the back of the shower.

I leaned back and let the water cascade over my breasts, my body tightening as I watched Frost kneel before me. His green gaze never left mine as he positioned himself between my legs, a wicked smirk playing at the corner of his lips as his hands circled my thighs and jerked me forward.

My pussy ached with the sudden intense need to be touched. I moaned as he licked a trail down the inside of my left thigh, clenching the tile ledge of the seat with white knuckles.

"Fuck, Frost," I managed between breathy moans.

He was *torturing* me, and he was enjoying it.

After another minute of playful nibbling and licking, I couldn't take it anymore. I released the ledge and took his head between my hands, the hot water from the shower-head pouring over my back. "Stop. Teasing," I told him in a growl and lowered his head to my throbbing sex.

He grinned at me before going to work. The instant his tongue settled on my clit, I convulsed with the urge to come. But I shoved the urge down. After all that teasing, I was going to make him work for it, at least a little.

Well, that was my intention. But the bastard was damn good at going down on a woman. His tongue circled me expertly, flicking and pressing and swirling all at the right times. When he added his fingers to the party, I was help-less to stop the quickening as it began to take over.

My muscles squeezed and my hips moved against his mouth almost of their own accord as I found my climax in a long, shaking moan.

Frost planted a kiss on my mound before lifted his head. "That's my girl," he said with a devious arch of his left brow, moving to stand so his cock was level with my mouth. He wrapped a hand around the back of my neck, securing it there with a fistful of my hair.

With lust-filled eyes and hard breaths, he stared down into my eyes and ordered in a husky voice, "*Open.*"

I did as I was told, parting my lips and leaning forward out of the spray of the water. Frost held my gaze as he pushed the head of his cock into my mouth. I welcomed him in, sliding my tongue around his tip. The hand he had fisted in my hair tightened and his body tensed.

He cursed under his breath as he slid out of my mouth and then back in slowly, testing how far he could go without choking me. Lucky for him, I'd never had a particularly touchy gag reflex. I took him deep into the back of my throat and he made a strained sound and shuddered.

"Christ, Rosie," he grunted, dragging his throbbing cock from my lips only to thrust it back in, harder this time, deeper.

The feel of him in my mouth. Of his strong hand holding my head in place. The strain of the hair at my scalp as he pulled and twisted. The sight of him gloriously naked and coated in slippery wetness. *Fuck.*

Urging him on, I moved my hands around the back of his thighs and prodded him faster, letting him fuck my mouth to his undoing. His movements became shakier by the second and I caught the exact moment he found his release, his face crumpling as he released my hair in favor of using the wall to hold himself up. "Fuck," he shouted as his saltiness coated my tongue and slid down my throat.

I swallowed him down as he pulled out and sighed, smiling down at me. His eyes traced a line down to my lips, further to my throat and eventually my hard, perky breasts. Lower to the tight muscle of my stomach and then the pulsing wetness of my pussy against the tile. His fangs slid free and I shuddered.

It seemed vampires weren't hindered in the staying hard department. Frost had only just begun to soften after having his release, but I could already feel him growing hard all over again.

Good. Because I was nowhere near finished with him.

I licked my lips and seductively opened my thighs to him, letting the water run down my chest. He growled and moving so fast I hardly saw him from all the steam, he gripped me by one arm and hauled me to my feet. I almost slipped, but Frost caught me, pressing me against my back against the wall.

This was not going to be gentle, his eyes warned.

Frost lifted my right leg, pulling my left foot to the tip of its toes to make me level with his cock. My fingernails dug into the hard flesh of his biceps as his wild eyes fixated on me—on the vein in my neck.

I gave him access, breathing heavily as I tipped my head to one side.

A low animal roar rumbled in his chest an instant before he struck. The sharp pain of his bite melding into agonizing pleasure as he drove his cock into me in one quick, *hard* thrust.

I gasped, barely able to adjust to his size before he was out and pushing in again, and then again. Harder with each thrust, pounding my pussy. Drilling me into the wall.

He suckled at my neck and as his venom mixed with my blood, my heartbeat quickened, and I could already feel myself tumbling headlong into orgasm.

Frost's large hands found my hips and held them tightly, his fingers digging into the flesh and bone so hard there I thought he might leave a bruise. He had me off the ground now, holding me suspended against the wall, my legs spread wide to grant him unrestricted access to my pussy.

My inner lioness roared, digging her fingernails so hard into Frost they began to draw blood. But he didn't seem to mind, and I was beyond caring about the bruising pressure of his fingertips. I could barely feel the pain because his bite was sedating me and bringing me to life all at once. And his quick, pounding thrusts against my pussy were driving me to a ledge there would be no coming back from.

He slowed for an instant and I cried out. "Don't you dare fucking stop," I managed through the delirium, and Frost quickened his pace, shoving us both over that ledge in a dizzying torrent of raw pleasure.

CHAPTER 9

$\mathcal{T}$he girl named Valentina awoke the next evening, only about an hour after I came downstairs for some water and a snack. I'd been watching her from an armchair in the living room while Ethan quietly worked on synthesizing more of my blood and marrow into a cure behind me.

It was different for everyone—how long the transition took. But it was clear as I watched her when it began in earnest. With each bite of my fucking amazing breakfast wrap Estelle made me, I saw the color return to her pale skin.

She'd been cleaned off and was wrapped in a fluffy white bathrobe, not unlike the one I was wearing right now. Her ankle was in a hard cast and she looked almost peaceful. At least until the final bit of the transition took her. Then she awoke gasping and clutching her chest, a quiet scream filtering past her lips as her new vampire eyes adjusted to the light.

She sat bolt upright, still pressing a hand to her chest, which was rising and falling rapidly with each labored breath. She muttered something in Italian I had to assume was some sort of curse.

"Do you speak english?" I asked and she turned to me, jumping back as though she could disappear into the couch cushions.

Valentina looked over me warily, studying my fluffy housecoat and bare feet. My sex rumpled hair and greasy wrap poised over my lips. Once she'd assessed I was no danger, she eyed Ethan and after deciding he was no immediate threat, either, her breathing began to level out. She raised her left hand to her mouth and pressed against two spots just above her upper lip, wincing.

"Those are your fangs," I explained. "They take some time to fully come in."

I hadn't known much about the transition, but while I waited for her to wake up, Ethan filled me in on all the little intricacies I didn't know. I'd only ever encountered one freshly made vampire before, so that was really all I had to go on.

Valentina massaged her gums and I noticed how very blue her eyes were. Like twin sapphires shot through with the golden light of the sun. She was incredibly pretty. "Fangs?" she repeated.

"So, you do speak English, then?"

She nodded slowly, removing her hand from her mouth to inspect her bathrobe. "Where are my clothes? What happened?"

Her words were lightly accented, but her English was

near flawless. For that I was grateful. It would have been a bitch to get Azrael to translate everything.

This was the part I was dreading. "You don't remember?"

She'd likely been compelled not to scream. But usually vampires didn't compel you to forget until *after* they fed. *Fear makes the blood taste sweeter*. Or at least, that was what one cocky vamp told me before I staked him in the heart.

A crease formed between Valentina's brows as she hung her head. After a minute, when her eyes became glassy, she looked up. "I do remember," she said and covered her mouth in horror. "What...what were they?"

I waited for her to piece it together. There was enough about vampires in popular culture that was true for her to be able to figure it out. At the very least, I was sure she'd have seen Twilight. She was right in that age demographic.

She gasped again and pressed her hand back to her chest. "But...but I'm not dead. I can—I can feel my heartbeat."

I shook my head, swallowing past the lump trying to form in my throat. "You won't be able to for very long," I explained, turning to look at Ethan for help explaining. I still didn't fully understand this bit. I didn't want to tell her she may not survive.

Ethan didn't look happy about my dragging him into it, but he stopped what he was doing and came to perch on the arm of the chair I was sitting in. I put a hand on his thigh in a silent thank you for not making me do it.

"Y-you're one of *them*," Valentina said, appraising him

closer up. "I—I can hear your heartbeat," she said, pointing to me as her breathing picked up again. "But he —*he* doesn't have one."

Fearful tears filled her eyes.

Ethan cleared his throat. "You're right. I don't. And soon you won't, either. It's a part of the transition. After dying," he explained, using vague hand gestures to help explain his point. "The body reanimates. The venom in a bite kick-starts the heart and accelerates the death process."

Her mouth fell open and I wasn't sure if it was because she didn't understand or because she was wishing she wasn't.

"No," she said, rising on unsteady feet. "No. This is a dream. Monsters are not real. *You* are not real. None of this is—"

"It is," I said in a hard voice. The sooner she accepted it, the better. Denying it wasn't going to help her any. "And I think you know that."

Her pouty bottom lip quivered, and she fell back down to sit on the couch with her head in her hands. Her sun-stained brown hair fell forward in waves to curtain off the pain in her face.

"It takes time to complete the transition for females. You will go through what others have described as accelerated menopause."

Ouch.

"And you will need to feed, a *lot*, to sustain yourself through the transition."

She looked up in horror. "Feed?"

I couldn't look at her anymore. I took the blood bag out of my lap where I'd been keeping it warm, wrapped in the folds of my housecoat. I tossed it to her, and it landed unceremoniously on the cushion next to her. A flicker of disgust crossed her features before the scent of it reached her nostrils and I watched her throat bob with a swallow.

"I can't drink that," she said, her accent growing thicker with her panic.

"You can and you will if you want to survive," I told her, setting down my wrap on the side table. I'd completely lost my appetite by this point. I rubbed my hands together as I bent over my knees, imploring her to understand what would happen if she tried to refuse.

"Women…" I began, trying to think of the best way to rip off the band aid. The poor girl had already died once, I didn't want to tell her she may very well die a second time and not come back. I sighed. "Female vampires are rare."

Her face went pale the instant I said the word vampire, as if she'd been afraid to accept that was the case.

Ethan stiffened under my hand. "They are rare because, for whatever reason, they don't always survive the transition. Somewhere along the line, their bodies often reject the change and…" Ethan trailed off.

He told me what happens to them. He'd seen it once, in a female they found undergoing the transition in Boulder. She'd grown cold and weak—that was the first sign. Then she began to cough up blood. No matter how much she drank, she became frail, as though her bones were losing density. She was in a massive amount of pain.

And then in the end, when they found her, she was

bleeding from every orifice in her body. Her eyes were completely bleached of color.

Valentina didn't need to know all that, though. "And when they reject the change, they die," I told her plainly without going into all the gory details. "Their hearts stop beating and they don't stay alive like Ethan here."

Her jaw clenched. "Maybe that would be best," she muttered, staring disgustedly at the blood bag.

I was inclined to agree. Once upon a time, I'd have locked myself up and let the transition kill me, or take my own life, before I tried to save myself only to live as something less than human.

But looking at Ethan and thinking of my guys, I wasn't so sure anymore. "That's your choice," I told her. "I'm so sorry this happened to you, Valentina."

"Val," she corrected sharply. "No one calls be Valentina except my mother..." her fists clenched and the tears that'd been welling in her eyes spilled over.

"Val," I acquiesced. "But you don't have to live your life like the bastards who did this to you."

She looked up at me hopefully, her eyes pleading. "How?"

I gestured to the blood bag. "Ethan," I said, squeezing his thigh. "And my other...*friends*," I paused, wondering what in the fuck to call them. Ethan's ears turned pink. "They survive on blood bags, which isn't as good as drinking from the vein from what I understand, but it does work. They also *hunt* vampires like the ones who took you and fed on you."

Some of the pain in her expression mellowed.

"And as a female, if you survive the change, you will inevitably become queen of your own vampire harem—if you choose to—and the vampire male's who follow you will need to follow *your* rules."

Her face broke. "I don't understand," she said in a breath, falling against the back of the couch. "Queens? Vampires? A *harem*? What does this all mean?"

"Rose," I heard the call from the doorway to the living room and turned to find Azrael standing there with his hands clasped behind his back. His expression unreadable as his gaze passed over the transitioning vampire in his house. "May I speak with you for a moment?"

I gave an apologetic smile to Ethan who nodded and turned back to Val. He slid into the seat I'd been occupying as I slid out and stood. "I'll answer any questions you have," he told the girl as I followed Azrael from the room.

"She survived," he mused as he led me down the hall, but we both knew she hadn't truly. Valentina was in limbo. Not quite living and not quite dead. Not quite human and not quite a vampire.

Only time would tell if she lived long enough to be remade as vampire, or if she would die while she still had a sliver of her humanity.

CHAPTER 10

*A*zrael had wanted to show me where the other vampire's we'd found in Naples were being kept. I finally found the purpose of all the blocked off old doorways and passages in the massive castle-like estate. They led to an older part of the building. An entirely separate wing.

"They've been compelled not to enter this part of the house, so you'll be safe so long as you're inside. I wanted to ask that you don't try to enter the west wing, and that if you are going outside that you are accompanied by at least one of your blood mates."

I stared incredulously at him. "My what?"

He squinted his eyes down at me as we turned away from the rusted shut doorway at the far end of the central part of the estate leading to the west wing. "That is what they are, isn't it? You may not be a vampire, but you are, in a way, *theirs*. You act as their queen would. Sustaining them, among other things…"

He wasn't wrong, but I didn't like the idea of him thinking I *belonged* to anyone. I also didn't like that he thought I needed protecting from the saddest looking bunch of vampires I'd ever seen.

Azrael's lips pulled up into a contemplative half-smile and I knew he'd read my thoughts. "They aren't as useless as we'd originally thought," he said with a hint of surprise coloring his tone. He stared at the closed off west wing as though he could see through it to the other side and the five vampires who were at this very moment, gorging on a never ending supply of blood bags, waiting for their promise of the sun tomorrow morning.

"One is a...what did he call it? A *hacker*, that's it. He can break into difficult computer and security systems."

That was pretty useful, I had to admit, especially since we knew that wherever Rafe was locked down tight with heavy vampire and computer security.

"And the tall gangly looking one," Azrael continued. "He spent a lot of time overseas...dismantling bombs. He assured me he also knows how to *make* them."

Ok, this was something.

"Guess we shouldn't judge a book by its cover then, hmm?" I said in a light tone and nudged his arm.

"No," he said, his face darkening as he looked down at me, forcing a chill to creep down the length of my spine. He was so close I could feel the *otherness* washing over me in waves. I could smell his unique scent of birch and sweet African violets. "I shouldn't."

With my throat suddenly tight, I took a step back and tried to shake off the shiver still trying to claw its way up to my scalp and down to my toes. The way he was looking at me was sending little shivers over my skin and I clenched my fists to ward off the feeling. His mismatched eyes narrowed on my face and my lips parted, wondering what he was thinking behind that beautiful mask he wore. His sharp cheekbones flared as his jaw clenched, and my mouth went dry.

"Was that all?" I asked him, trying to change my train of thought so he wouldn't hear the little minx yawning awake, or see any of the images she was throwing against the backs of my eyelids every time I blinked. I turned away from him, ready to go back down to the makeshift lab and check on Val—make sure she was at least trying to feed. But he stopped me.

Azrael's hand circled my wrist and yanked me back. I didn't have time for my brain to catch up, or for my attack reflex to kick in before he kissed me.

His lips pressed hard against mine, shocking all the breath from my lungs in a gasp. My eyelids fluttered as he moved his lips against mine, finding the spot where they fit against each other just right. A warmth burst into my chest and fanned out to my stomach, making my toes curl and my belly ache.

His fingers played at the base of my neck, gently holding there, as though afraid to break me. I moaned as he slid his tongue in and my body reacted to him, pushing into him. Sparks flying from every nerve ending as though he'd set me on fire.

But as his lips opened, the air rushed back into my lungs and reality swept in with it in a massive punch to my gut. I bit down and Azrael groaned, backing away while staring up at me in shock, his bottom lip bleeding from where I'd bit him.

I tasted his blood in my mouth and he wiped the crimson dribble from his chin, breathless as he held my gaze.

There was hurt in his eyes. And fury. But mostly I saw pain. I saw a deep pain-filled longing that made my own heart clench in my chest, making it hard to breathe.

Before either of us could say anything, I spun and ran down the hall. I didn't stop until I was in my room, slamming the door shut behind me as I slumped against it in horror of what I'd just allowed to happen.

I kicked the edge of the bed over and over until the sting brought me back to earth. I cursed, gritting my teeth.

What the fuck was I doing?
What the fuck had I just done?

CHAPTER 11

*I*gnoring a problem doesn't make it go away.

But it was the easiest option. Over the next couple of days, as Valentina slowly got used to her new reality, and Blake, Frost, Azrael, and I gathered more vampires to our cause, it seemed Azrael was equally happy to pretend it never happened.

Thank fuck for that because I really didn't know what I'd say to him if he asked about it. *He'd* kissed *me.* But...I'd *definitely* kissed him back. And if I was being *really* honest with myself; I enjoyed it.

I shuddered, stepping back over the threshold into the house with the guys trailing behind me, bloodstained and tired, but alright. We exterminated two vampire nests during the night, and managed to convince one to join us, which brought our numbers up to somewhere around twenty-five. Pitiful, but we were getting somewhere, albeit *very* slowly.

There were only so many nests in the surrounding

cities of Italy. Azrael said we'd have to take his jet and start sourcing from other countries if we were going to be able to get the numbers we needed. So, we were going on a three-day trip back to the states to gather as many as we could and bring them back here.

We had until sunset to get ready to leave. If Azrael's intel was right, Raphael was starting to get restless. Apparently, he'd hired a witch of his own and was actively searching for me. Azrael hardly allowed me to step foot outside without him on my heels anymore. Amala's wards around the house were holding, and she assured us they would continue to hold as long as she was living, but the warding spells she cast over me for when we left the house didn't last more than several hours before the magic holding them to my skin faded.

I wasn't too worried, though. With Azrael by my side, I knew that even if Raphael himself came for me, this time Az would do what he should have done in the streets of Baton Rouge. He would finally put an end to his brother's terror.

Or at least, that was what I was banking on. And I welcomed it. All the better if we could kill the bastard and avoid this whole stupid thing. I mean, would Rafe *actually* try to become some fucked up version of a king over the mortal race? It sounded pretty outlandish to me.

"It isn't outlandish when you can compel all the world leaders to bend the knee..." Azrael said in a deadly tone as he followed me down the hallway toward Ethan's lab.

"What?" I barked, spinning on my heel to face him. "What the hell are you talking about?"

Azrael's unwavering stare fixed on my face and a muscle in his jaw twitched. "It's what I think he's planning to do. There's a—what do you call it?—one of those meetings between your world leaders in two months' time. If he can find out the location and get inside, which we both know he can, then he would have everything he needed to complete his mission."

My stomach dropped. "He would do that?"

Azrael grimaced. "He believes we are the dominant species. In his mind, it's the way it should be. Humans bowing to the power of immortals, offering up their own as sacrifices to feed our race. Offering immortality to those who *he* deems deserving of it. He imagines a world where he is king."

At this point, Blake and Frost had caught up with us, and Ethan and Val came out of the lab to join us in the hall.

"He's had his sights set on this for a long time," Azrael added, running a wide hand over the back of his thick neck. "But it's been hundreds of years. I never thought he would actually follow through with it. I thought…"

I clenched my jaw, hating to see the pain in Azrael's eyes, but right now the anger was outweighing my empathy. "You thought you could change his mind. That you could save him."

Azrael glanced up and I saw the ache within him. "I did."

Blake and Frost cursed in tandem, their faces hardening.

Azrael swallowed and licked his lips. "But I don't

anymore. He's beyond saving. I know that now," he sighed. "And he's never been closer to attaining his goal. If we don't stop him now, it will be too late."

We were all silent for a moment while we allowed the new information to sink in. Azrael's intel could be wrong about what Raphael was planning, but even if it was, who was to say he didn't have some other equally terrifying plan? That was the thing about being immortal...it was only a matter of time. If left alive, eventually Raphael would succeed.

Val's voice broke through the silence and I turned to find her standing resolute next to Ethan, her small hands clasped into fists at her sides. Her jaw set. "I've decided I want to help," she said. "In whatever way I can."

I smiled at her. She was really coming into her own. After the first day and night spent basically in solitude, grieving for what she'd lost, she seemed to be coming out of it stronger than I could've ever imagined. I recognized the glint of fire and steel in her bright blue eyes. She was using anger to fuel her.

Maybe not the smartest motivator, but who was I to judge? Isn't that what I'd allowed to motivate me since I was just a teenager, sharpening my very first stakes. I turned out okay, for the most part. She would be fine, too.

"Thank you," I told her earnestly, and then moved to go with her and Ethan into the lab, turning to tell Frost and Ethan that I would meet them upstairs soon and they could use the shower first.

"How are you feeling?" I asked Valentina as I walked into the sitting room. I glanced back to see if Azrael had followed me, but he was gone. I gulped and found a bare patch of wall of lean against, crossing my arms over my chest as I allowed my gaze to rove over her. "You look okay."

She nodded. "I feel okay."

I turned to Ethan. "What do you think, doc? She going to make it?"

Ethan smirked from his spot behind the lab desk and nodded. "Yes. I think she will be. If the change was going to kill her, there should be signs by now."

Val and I shared a smile.

A few days ago, she said she'd rather die than become like the monsters who took away her mortality. I was glad that she'd changed her mind—even if the only real reason she did was to get revenge. There were worse motivators.

"Can I come with you?" She asked suddenly. "Ethan says you're all going to the United States to rally more vampires. I want to help."

I winced. "It isn't...safe," I tried, not wanting her to feel offended. "Newborn vampires aren't as strong as older ones. And you have no training. We can fix that. In fact, I'd be happy to train you when we get back. But for now, honestly Val, you'd just get yourself killed."

She frowned and that lick of fire in her eyes dimmed.

"It's not forever," I added. "You *will* get your revenge. Just not yet."

She nodded solemnly and dropped her gaze, wandering out the doorway at the back of the sitting room toward the kitchen. I sighed and walked over to

Ethan, turning back to make sure she was out of earshot. "Is she okay around Estelle?"

"Yeah. She feeds regularly, and even if she didn't, Azrael compelled her not to feed from or harm Estelle or Jen."

"Jen?"

"She's the other mortal who helps Estelle sometimes."

I vaguely remembered seeing her the first day I awoke here. "Oh."

Ethan set down the petri dish he was dropping some sort of liquid in and turned to meet my gaze. "How are *you* doing?"

I managed a small smirk. "I'm doing okay."

He snaked an arm around my waist and my smile grew. Warmth spread through my chest as he pressed his nose against mine, the dimples in his cheeks growing more pronounced as he smirked. "I've been missing you," he purred, fingering the exposed flesh at my lower back.

A soft whimper escaped my lips as that slow ache Ethan was so good at evoking from me pooled in my belly, making my toes curl. With his warm body pressed against me, all my worries seemed further away, and I melted into his arms, wrapping my arms around his shoulders.

"I've missed you, too."

While I'd been busy hunting and gathering, he'd been busy synthesizing and studying. Each of the vampires save for the newest recruits had now had a taste of the sun and they were eager to do anything we wanted them to get another.

Azrael was right, the sun had been the *perfect* motivator. If they weren't before, each of them was now *firmly* on our side against Raphael.

Gathering vampires from the states might prove more difficult, though, and I was sort of glad Ethan would be staying behind for the trip. In the states, vampires knew who I was. They knew of The Black Rose. It would be harder to rally them.

But there were so many there, and there wasn't a language barrier. Azrael could speak eleven languages, but five of those were ancient dialects no one on this earth spoke anymore. We'd run out of ground to cover in Europe pretty quick.

Ethan brought me back to him with a tiny kiss on the tip of my nose. My cheeks flushed. "Stay," he whispered against my lips. "I could use some help here in the lab, and Azrael and the guys have this. You don't have to go."

I swallowed hard, pulling my bottom lip in between my teeth to keep from groaning as his cock hardened between us, pressing against my bellybutton. "*So* not fair," I whispered back playfully, running my fingers through his soft golden hair.

"I never said I would play fair," he growled before pressing his lips to mine. I gasped and my fingers turned to claws in his hair, pulling him hard against me.

His lips parted and I let him in, that warm ache spreading like wild fire through my veins until I was shivering from it. Everywhere he touched me shot sparks into my blood to spur the flames. He groaned against my mouth and the sound reverberated like thunder in my own chest.

Ethan's scent of nautical cologne and fresh mint filled my nose and body responded, legs pressing together, chest rising and falling more rapidly with each fevered kiss. After a moment he broke away, breathless, and pressed his forehead to mine. "Stay," he whispered again.

"You know I can't," I replied, wanting to hold him against me for as long as I could.

He sighed loudly and pulled back just enough to see into my eyes. "You could," he urged.

I shook my head.

"I…" he struggled to find the words. "I have this horrible feeling in my gut," he said finally, pain his tone and drawing down the corners of his eyes. "It sounds stupid, I know, but—"

I cupped his face, forcing him to look at me. "It isn't stupid," I told him. It wasn't stupid to worry about me. I worried about him, and about all my guys every goddamned day. But I was grateful Ethan was *here*. At least him I didn't have to worry about. For now, anyway.

He offered me a halfhearted grin and planted a swift kiss on my forehead before pulling away. "Promise me you'll be careful," he asked, his voice sharp now. He wasn't playing around anymore. He wanted my word.

I but my bottom lip.

"Please," he added after a minute. "Don't go pulling any shit like you did in Naples with Val."

I opened my mouth to argue, but he held up a hand to silence me.

"Rose. I know you can take care of yourself. I'm not doubting that. But for *my* own sanity—because I'm selfish and the only way I can keep working is if I know you'll be safe—just do this for me. Promise me you won't go looking for trouble. You'll listen to Azrael if he says something isn't safe. You'll let *him* deal with shit if it comes up. Can you promise me that?"

His steeped tea eyes bored into me, waiting for my response. I tried to imagine what it would be like if the tables were turned to unruffle my feathers. I didn't like to be controlled. I didn't like to be told what to do. But if it was Ethan going instead of me, wouldn't I ask of him the same thing he was asking of me now?

Swallowing my pride, I resigned myself to his request. I could let Azrael take the lead on this one, couldn't I? It was only three days. I could be careful for three days, couldn't I? I could behave.

Even I didn't believe my own lies, but if I made this promise, I wouldn't break it.

"I can't promise you that," I said finally and watched Ethan's face harden. "But I can promise you that I will *try* to. *Really try*. Does that work?"

Ethan's expression softened and he hugged me to him, tucking my head into the crook of his shoulder as he kissed my crown. "Yeah, baby. That'll work."

CHAPTER 12

I slept fitfully through that afternoon. You'd think the glorious fucking the guys had given me after we'd all showered would have knocked me into a coma. But Ethan's worry had set me on edge.

It was silly. I knew everything was going to be fine. I would make sure of it. But my mother's words to live by were always *trust your gut.* My gut wasn't telling me I was in any more imminent danger than I always was on a daily basis. But Ethan's gut was telling him otherwise. I turned back to my left side for the hundredth time and Frost shifted in the bed beside me.

If I kept this up, I would end up waking them all up. With a hushed sigh, I slid from the warmth of their bodies and the covers and tugged my fluffy housecoat over my naked body, wandering into the hall.

I needed a distraction. I was already all packed up and all that was left to do was fill a few more plastic bags with my blood for Ethan, give him a healthy marrow sample, and get dressed to leave. But we weren't scheduled to take off from the runway for another four hours. And the semi-private airstrip Azrael used was only thirty minutes away. I found myself wandering nearer the back of the house after finding the kitchen devoid of life and Valentina sleeping soundly on the sofa in the lab. She had her own room but seemed always to gravitate back to that central spot of the house where she awoke.

With the house as quiet as it was in the hours before dusk, it was almost eerie. The crown molding looked oppressive rather than pretty. The shadows seemed darker. The hallways narrower.

I tip toed down a corridor toward the west wing. I'd seen the corridor before, but it looked like it dead-ended at another door with a rusted shut bolt, so I'd never bothered to go down it.

But now I could feel a difference in the air in that direction and peered more closely into the dim to see that there was an open archway set into the wall on the left further down, closer to the door to the west wing. Curious, I crept to the opening and peeked around the edge, finding that there was a light on somewhere down the curving stone staircase.

Interest piqued, I made my way down the steps, sucking in a breath as my bare feet left the carpet to connect with chilled, rough stone. After descending for a minute or so, I figured I had to be pretty far underground. My breath clouded the air and I wrapped my arms around myself, trying to rub some warmth back into my bones.

The air was stagnant and musty, like it had been back at the cave where Azrael had kept me not so long ago. I almost turned back, my claustrophobia rearing its ugly head, pooling my stomach with unease. I hunched inward, as though the walls were a physical weight on my body. But, there, just ahead, the passageway forked off in two directions.

One was dark and quiet, the only sound emanating from it the steady dripping of water from some unseen source. The other was lit with a dim light that was clearly really far away, but it was there.

So was the faint sound of piano. The notes slow but gaining momentum. It was a haunting tune and my heart squeezed at the sad sound of it. I knew at once that it had to be Azrael.

Who else would be holed up underground playing a fucking piano?

I hesitated, unsure if I wanted to see him. But surely by now he would know I was here. And if that weren't enough, it was as though the music was pulling me in. Tugging on something deep in my core that I didn't know was there.

My eyes stung as I moved further into the stone passageway and I grit my teeth against my body's urge to turn and run in the opposite direction. To turn and run until my lungs could breathe fresh air again. But I needed to see it. I wanted to hear the music without the dulling of distance and stone.

I found myself coming up on an opening in the passage after a minute of forced walking. The music was so loud now that I could feel it like a physical thing in my chest, as though the notes were being played on my ribcage instead of the ivory keys at Azrael's fingertips.

He sat at the massive piano, shirtless, with bare feet. Only a pair of low-riding dark jeans clung to his legs. I was wrong, I didn't think he had any idea I was there. He played expertly, entirely lost in the music. His head swayed as he played. His eyes were firmly closed. Every muscle in his wide back and shoulders was flexed. He was using everything inside him to play.

It was so beautiful it made me want to cry, but that was stupid, wasn't it? Who cried because they thought a song was beautiful? I mean, did people actually do that? Or was that just something that happened in movies?

My throat burned, but I managed to keep myself in check, watching him in raptured silence as the song eventually hit its massive crescendo and then slowed, the melody evening out, growing fainter. The notes more spaced out until the last deep note rang out, holding in the air like the breath I was holding in my lungs.

I must have made some sort of sound, because Azrael whirled on the stool to face me, his face pale and eyes wild and wide. A snarl echoed in the wide cavern-like space and he was upon me faster than I could blink. My back met stone and I cried out as it dug into a spot between my shoulder blades.

My arms were pinned above my head and he roared, looking every bit the monster I once thought he was. His fangs long and shining in the dim light. His face horrifically twisted in pain and rage.

This time, I didn't cower. I stared at him, defiant. Unwilling to bend to his desire to frighten me.

His breaths slowed and his expression relaxed in slow increments, as though he was coming out of some sort of trace. Coming back to himself with each slow blink of his beautiful eyes.

Azrael's fangs retracted and his grip on me loosened, but he didn't release me. His eyes darted left and right, confused as he found his way back to reality from the daze that'd taken him. "What are you doing down here?" he breathed, his voice stained with the remnants of his fury.

I struggled for words. "I—I couldn't sleep," I swallowed to try to get some moisture back into my dry throat. "I heard you playing and…"

And I couldn't turn away, I finished in my mind, unable to voice it because it didn't make sense even to me.

His gaze softened.

"Can you," I hedged, glancing at his hands still holding mine firm against the jagged stone. "My hands are going numb."

He blinked and dropped my arms. I rubbed the sore spots on my wrists and coughed to clear my throat. "I didn't mean to um…*interrupt* anything."

I wasn't really sure what to say now that the music had stopped. But it was almost like I could still feel the memory of it in the air. Like the reverberation of the haunting notes were trapped in the stone.

For the first time, I took a wide sweep of the space. Finding something like a bedroom set up around the piano at the middle of it. A large bed to the right and a worn brown couch and coffee table further away. A fireplace glowing with the remnants of a fire that was burning a good hour before to the left, a massive store of wine next to it. The bottles set into holes bored into the stone wall itself. There had to be at least three hundred bottles from the floor to the twenty-foot ceiling.

"You really have a thing for caves, huh?" I asked, trying to lighten the mood in the oppressive space. At least here it wasn't as tight as in the corridor. My body still rebelled at the lack of immediate exits and fresh air, but the width and height made it more tolerable.

Azrael stepped back as I stepped forward to get a better look at the space. I walked around the piano and toward the fire and the wall of wine, hoping the embers in the stone hearth still held some warmth. My toes felt damn near ready to fall off from the icy floor.

A gilt frame caught my eye and I crooked my neck to look at it. Above the hearth was a portrait of a woman. It was old. At least a few hundred years, if not more. She had to be in her mid-twenties, though she could have been younger.

It wasn't like the usual art pieces of women from that era. She didn't have one of those weird collar things sticking out, or the big hair all pinned and twirled elaborately atop her head. She was simple. She was stunning.

It was a front profile, but the woman had her face turned slightly away from the artist, showing off her long neck and a beautiful side profile of her high cheekbones and pert nose, though it obscured the color of her eyes.

She had long waving reddish brown hair, but the color was faded to a dull shade from the passage of time.

A necklace that looked suspiciously like a rosary disappeared into the dark crevasse between her breasts. *Nice* breasts. Like, *really nice breasts.* Or maybe it was the way the corset she was wearing pressed against them that made them look impossibly perky.

"Who is she?" I found myself asking in a whisper before consciously making the decision to speak. She had a sort of haunting beauty, and I felt I needed to know who this was and why Azrael had a painting of her in his bedroom…

I jumped as Azrael appeared beside me, spooked out of my reverie.

He gazed up at her with equal measures of adoration and agony and I realized that this wasn't just some painting in an old castle-like estate. He *knew* her.

Of course, he knew her. He was a thousand goddamned years old.

"Her name was Annabella."

Azrael's voice was scratchy and strained around the name. He didn't offer anything else other than her name, but it was easy to guess the rest.

He loved her.

She died.

I wondered how…

Azrael turned his gaze away from the portrait and looked down at me curiously. "Of old age," he said in a gruff whisper. "As it should be."

I could barely contain my surprise, my mind trying to fill in the massive blanks of the story.

Azrael bent to toss a log into the hearth, and I noticed something in his face harden as the embers flared from the disturbance. "So, you see, dear Rose; you were wrong. I *have* loved, and it was the worst thing I ever did."

My heart squeezed in my chest.

I knew what it was like to lose someone. But this was different. This was a love Azrael had chosen. And despite the fact that I'm sure he would have loved to spend the rest of eternity with the woman he was now staring at with a hurricane of emotion on his face, he didn't force immortality on her. I wondered if he left her once she was sagging and wrinkled, or if—

He turned on me with that flicker of mad fury I'd glimpsed in him only a handful of times, his fangs bared to me again. This time I flinched. "I stayed with her until the very end," he growled at me. "Until she was cold and lifeless in my arms," his jaw twitched. "And longer," he continued in a barely there whisper. "Until she was stiff and rotting."

I shuddered.

"I would not wish *love* on anyone," he hissed, spitting the word as though it tasted vile on his tongue.

It took a moment for Azrael to calm himself, staring at me with his shoulders tense and stare piercing, as though waiting for me to give him a reason to strike out.

I quieted my mind, not wanting the headache of having to reset any of my bones before we could even leave the house.

His furrowed brows released their tension and he unhunched his frame, lips parting. "Do you really think I would intentionally hurt you?"

I lifted a brow. "Wouldn't you?"

He ran a hand over the shadow of scruff on his jaw. "No," he said. "I wouldn't."

But I didn't think even *he* believed that. He may not *intend* to—as he so eloquently put it—but there was a darkness in him. A shadowy pit of rage that could blind him to his own violence.

I knew because I had one of those pits within me to. An abyss that no light could ever hope to brighten. I didn't go there often. Not anymore. But I'd been there. I'd *lived* there for almost two years before I got my fucking head straight.

"I should probably go get dressed," I managed, feeling as though I was speaking around a mouthful of marbles.

My mind was at war with my mouth. There was no reason for me to stay. *I should go.* But a part of me wanted to stay. To tell Azrael that he was wrong. Without finding my guys again, I would have agreed with him. But not anymore.

You're wrong, I think, in the off chance he might be listening to my thoughts.

His eyes briefly flicker to mine and away again.

Love is *worth it. It's worth the pain. It's worth the grief. Loving Annabella wasn't the worst thing you ever did. I think it might have been the best...*

I took a tentative step away, half of my hoping he

hadn't heard what I couldn't say aloud, and the other half praying he had and that he believed it.

"Wait," he said, and I paused mid-step, tucking my housecoat tighter around my chilled flesh.

Azrael's lips tightened into a thin line and my throat tightened. Why couldn't I stop looking at his lips? Why for the last three days every time I saw him, I remembered how he kissed me? I couldn't get it out of my head and believe me *I've tried.*

"If it bothers you so much, why not ask me to compel you to forget?"

My jaw tightened.

"Or is it not that my kiss bothered you?" his eyes glittered with mischief and malice. "Is it that you *enjoyed* it?"

I parted my lips to respond. Curled my hand into a fist to punch him. But did neither, my breathing coming faster as he stepped in closer. Close enough that his scent fogged my mind and the nearness of him bristled my skin, charging the empty air between us.

"I don't know," I replied honestly, hating that it was the truth. I should've been afraid of him. *Hated* him. I should want to see his head on a pike. But I understood his darkness. And *my* darkness recognized its likeness in another being. An ancient, terrible, beautiful being.

I couldn't hate him no matter how much I wished I could.

Azrael lifted a hand to run a smooth thumb over my cheekbone and back further until his fingers pushed into my hair. My skin was on fire everywhere he was touching it. A haze fell over my eyes.

"Then maybe I should try it again," he said in a faint growl, and this time he didn't take me by surprise. This time I had every warning—every opportunity—to back away, and I didn't.

Azrael pressed his lips against mine, not roughly like he had three days ago. Softly. Like he was giving me the chance to change my mind. But as my body responded, he deepened the kiss, eliciting a delicious shiver from my spine.

A soft moan liberated itself from the tomb of my chest and he growled, pulling me tight against him until our bodies were melded together as one. His hand slid down my back, wrapping firmly at my lower waist as he lifted me onto him.

His arms were hard bars of unyielding muscle around me as I hooked my ankles behind his back, my body moving of its own accord, pressing my naked pussy against the growing bulge in his pants.

My hands came around his neck, fingers exploring the soft brown hair on the back of his head. He dipped his mouth lower, leaving mine to press a line of hot, insistent kisses down my jaw and along the side of my neck. The shock of hard fangs pressing against my skin broke me out of the trance and I pulled back from him, practically jumping out of his arms.

I scrambled to my feet, chest heaving, and blinking to clear my thoughts. "I—I'm sorry, I just—"

I just *what?*

His gaze clouded and all at once Azrael transformed

from a raw version of himself back into the stoic, closed off form that he used as a shield against the world.

"You just *what?*"

His sharp tone cut through me, and a spark of anger lit the reserves of kindling I kept in the darkness.

This wasn't fair. He wasn't being fair. I had my guys. They wouldn't be alright with this. They would *hate* this.

They would hate me.

Azrael couldn't expect me to just…

To just…

"Feel what you're feeling?" he asked, his voice dripping acid.

Finally finding my voice, I straightened, thinking this time I might actually hit him.

"You made it *very* clear that you no longer have the capacity to care for another living soul," I spat at him. He'd said it himself, hadn't he? That loving another person was the worst thing he ever did? So, then what the hell was he playing at?

It hurt to look at him as the realization sunk in. This was only about one thing, then…it wasn't at all what I thought it was. I wanted to laugh at myself for acting so foolishly. I chuckled darkly under my breath.

Fool me once…

"And I don't know if I gave you the wrong impression," I said in a tone rife with haughty disdain. "But if you're looking for a place to stick your dick, go find yourself a nice Italian prostitute. I'm not a toy to be played with, *Azrael*. And *this*," I said while gesturing to my pussy beneath the robe. "Is *not* a fucking vending machine for good times."

He shrugged. "Could've fooled me."

Motherfucker.

I took the two steps to close the space between us and slapped him hard across the face, fuming so badly my body shook and I would've been surprised if there wasn't steam coming out of my goddamned ears. So, when he caught my hand an inch away from its intended target, it only made me even more spitting mad.

Trembling, I wrenched my hand from his grasp. "Fuck you."

Something I couldn't name crossed his face. He released my hand and my nostrils flared as I pushed my right leg back, ready to put my entire body into the swing when he said, "I'm sorry," shocking me so completely that I forgot what I'd been about to do.

I deflated inch by inch until I was made up of nothing more than wasted rage and the heavy drag of spent adrenaline.

"I shouldn't have said that. It wasn't fair. I know how you feel about them," he glanced up toward the ceiling as though he could see my guys through the fifty feet of stone. "And how they feel about you."

My shoulders slumped.

It actually knows how to apologize...

Azrael smirked. "It does."

Oh my god stay out of my head!

"You're an asshole, you know that right?"

His lips pursed and he glanced away. It was as much of an admission as I was going to get.

"Since you've been *avoiding* me for three days, you're out of practice," he said, tactfully changing the subject. I had to admit I was more than a little grateful.

Azrael and I had been spending a little bit of time each day working on my mental barriers. I'd gotten better at blocking him out, but only when I was seriously focusing. If anything broke my concentration, my walls would slip, and he'd crash right in.

I still had yet to compel him to do anything, no matter how hard I tried, all I managed was making his eye twitch and once, when I told him to punch himself in the face, to make his fingers curl. But that was about the extent of it.

I also couldn't resist his compulsion worth shit.

And I wasn't able to pick up on a single one of *his* thoughts, no matter how hard I tried to *open my mind.*

Azrael nudged his head in the direction of the couch and table on the other end of the room. "We still have a few hours until dark. Think you can channel all that anger into something useful? Maybe keep that wall up for more than thirty seconds?"

The dick—he knew I couldn't say no when he phrased it as a damned challenge. I groaned. "Fine. But if I manage to block you for a full minute, then I want something."

His brows lowered as his face twisted into an apprehensive scowl. "What?"

"A burger."

"*What?*"

"You heard me. I want a burger. There's this little diner

I love in Baltimore that makes this *epic* fucking quarter pounder with Monterey Jack cheese, jalapenos, crispy fried onions, and this smokey barbeque sauce that is literally *to die for*."

The twitch of a smile played at the corner of his mouth. He nodded. "Deal."

"Then let's do this shit. You'll be wanting to give the pilot some notice of a change in flight plans."

CHAPTER 13

To say things were awkward between Azrael and I would be putting it lightly. As much as I tried to forget our kiss belowground in his cave room, I couldn't put it out of my head. Nor could I forget the things he said to me. The fact that I fucking *beat* his ass in our little bet helped take some of the edge off, though.

Turned out a well-seasoned chunk of beef was all it took to motivate me. He made note of that for our next training session and has promised me that if I can withstand him trying to batter down my defenses for *three* minutes that I will get an entire box of cupcakes from Crème de la Cake in San Francisco, my all-time favorite cake shop.

"Why can't we go now?" I whined as we settled into our seats on the private plane. "I'm hungry and you promised."

I opened my legs to Azrael, making a show of the fact

that I was armed and dangerous, my stakes glinting in the low lighting on the aircraft.

He rolled his eyes. "We have work to do."

"But you said—"

"I've added a stop in Baltimore to the flight plan for the return trip just to get you a *burger*, I'd say that I've made good on my bargain." He tossed me a few packs of pretzels and peanuts. "Here," he said coyly. "Have some nuts."

I snickered at him but tore open the top of the plastic film and dumped some pretzels into my mouth. "They're stale," I said around a mouthful of *yuck*.

Azrael shrugged. "I don't usually have mortal company aboard my plane."

Speaking of the plane, it was somehow *smaller* than I thought it would be. Not a full-size aircraft as I'd pictured since the last time, I was on it I was unconscious for the entirety of the trip. There were two banks of four seats. Each bank of four split into two against opposing walls facing each other. I was sitting across from Blake, who was staring out into the night with a crease between his brows.

"Hey," I said, kicking out to get his attention with a nudge to his seat. "What's up? You okay?"

He nodded slowly. "Yeah," he said and then shook his head, sending the longer strands of his dark hair brushing over his brow. "Fine. Just don't like flying."

I got the feeling that wasn't all but didn't want to press him. When Blake got all broody like he was now it was generally best to leave him alone.

Frost was sitting in the bank of four seats behind me, so the back of his chair was against the back of mine. I spun to see that he was alright as the plane began to drive along the curving path of the road in the field, leading us toward the runway.

Before I could ask him if he was good, I watched his fist clench against the plush leather seat and he asked, "Where were you this morning?" his voice gruff and gravelly.

I froze for an instant, my throat tightening. My gaze flickered to Azrael on the other side of the plane and I prayed Blake hadn't noticed. I was going to tell them about what happened between Azrael and I, even if it didn't ever go anywhere and it wouldn't happen again, they still deserved to know.

But not right now. Not when they needed to be at the top of their game. We had no idea what we were walking into in Phoenix. They had to have clear heads and not be worried about something between Azrael and I that was over and done with. Dead in the water. Total caputs.

"I was with Azrael," I told him without turning around to face him, careful not to look Blake in the eye, either. I infused the lie with truth. "We were practicing keeping up my mind barriers."

I chanced a peek at Blake from beneath my lashes. "You guys haven't done that in a few days," he mused, the words not really meriting a response, but I felt compelled to give one, anyway, prodded by guilt.

"Yeah. I needed the extra practice. Lasted a full minute, too. That's why he owes me the burger. It was a bet."

Blake pursed his lips, looking between Azrael and I. Seeming to decide something, he shrugged, and I saw his shoulders relax a bit as he slouched in his chair. "Well, I want one of those burgers. It they are as good as you said, maybe I'll actually be able to keep it down."

It was another sad truth of vampirism. Once you got a taste for blood, human food lost a lot of its flavor. It either tasted bland to them, or completely vile. There was very little in-between. And on the edible end of the spectrum was anything made from red meat. A burger cooked rare might actually taste alright for them.

I managed a watery smile and promised to have Azrael buy one for each of them. "Do we know where we're going first?" I asked Az as the plane lifted from the runway with a bumping jolt that lifted us from the earth. My stomach pressed against my spine and I eyed Blake from the corner of my eye, trying to gauge if he was alright.

His face was paler than usual, but as the plane leveled out, so did his pallor.

Before Azrael could answer me, I stood up and gestured for Blake to do the same. "Here, switch with me," I told him, holding out my hand to him. "It probably isn't helping that you're facing the back of the plane. Face forward. It might be better."

He gulped, but did as I suggested, unbuckling his seat-belt to switch sides with me so carefully it seemed like he expected the floor to fall out from beneath his feet.

"Better?" I asked him as I squirmed to find a comfortable position in his seat.

He nodded his thanks and then went back to brooding with his gaze fixed on the clouds outside the window. Frost looked like he'd passed out behind Blake and I smiled. He really could sleep anywhere... but I sure as hell wasn't going to be the one to wake him up. He was grumpy as hell after a nap unless he woke up on his own.

"So," I said quietly, turning in my seat to face Azrael again. "What's the plan?"

"Hmm?" he said, blinking as he turned to me. I wondered what he'd been thinking about.

I repeated the question.

"There are three good sized nests that I know of in the city, all within relative close proximity to one another. I thought we'd start with those and then branch out if we have time."

"More information from your *"intel"*," I asked, putting the word in air quotes.

He narrowed his gaze at me, and his chest rumbled with a *hmm* sound that I took to mean *yes.*

I flipped my hair back over my shoulder and cocked my head at him. "You ever going to tell us where you get all this information from?"

"Maybe," he said. "Maybe not."

I shook my head at him and leaned back against the headrest of the seat, letting my heavy eyelids flutter closed. I clasped my hands over my belly and sighed. The brain workout with Az this morning had really tired me out. "How long until we get to Phoenix?" I asked him.

"Long," he said cryptically as I felt the pull of exhaustion begin to lure me into its embrace. "And we'll be stuck in the hangar until sundown for a few hours, too."

"Mhmmm," I murmured, not even really sure what he was saying anymore.

"Sleep well, dear Rose."

WE DID GOOD IN PHOENIX ON THE FIRST NIGHT. WE HIT two of the three nests Azrael was aware of and managed to get an entire one to join us. Twelve new recruits from there. And three from the other nest. The rest wished to remain neutral. It was the first time a part of the nest left their kin behind and I was just as taken aback as the guys were.

Generally, once you'd found your place in a nest, with a queen, you didn't leave. Not ever. Not until you were dead.

I attributed our success to the fact that none of them seemed to know who I was. I didn't hit the southern states that often, though, so though I thought I doubtful, it was very possible they hadn't even heard of me.

So, in total we had fifteen, and they were all being put up in a large warehouse Azrael owned—one of many apparently. He'd allotted them an allowance to convert the warehouse to a livable space. There was already running water, but the vampires would at the very least need beds and a refrigeration system to store the blood bags Az promised them. He would meet them for an hour tonight to give them their promised dosage of the serum which he'd brought a small store of with us from Italy.

Hopefully that and the supply of blood would be enough to keep them with us.

The fact that he seemed to have a never-ending supply of the stuff was not lost on me, and I cringed thinking of all the people chivalrously donating their blood and time to help other mortals, only for their efforts to be diverted into the hungry mouths of immortals. But drinking from a blood bag was better than killing people.

And unlike what my guys did to themselves on purpose to avenge me, I was starting to realize there were many vampires who never asked for the life they now had. They were turned against their will. Or left for dead only to survive and wake as something other than human.

One of the women in the nest we convinced to come to our side just yesterday had cancer before she changed. It was *why* she attempted the transition when she found out the man she was dating was actually a vampire. It was that or accept her terminal diagnosis and die slowly. Now she was alive and thriving. The queen of a good-sized nest.

How could I blame her for doing what was necessary to save her life?

If I had to make the same choice, what would I choose?

All the lines I'd drawn over the years were being irrevocable blurred. Some erased entirely. There was a large part of me that still cringed at the whole ordeal, but there was another part—a part steadily growing larger— that was beginning to understand.

I wasn't sure if I liked it.

I shuddered, sipping my coffee as I pulled a tray of

bacon out of the oven and lifted the strips of greasy goodness onto a plate lined with paper towels.

"Just bacon?" Frost asked, staring down the sharp line of his nose at me, one eyebrow raised.

"And coffee," I corrected him. "There's at least three food groups there."

He smirked.

Blake was still asleep in one of the two rooms connected to the main living space that contained this tiny kitchenette and a sunken in square of carpet with a sectional couch and a coffee table. It was another place Azrael owned. Blake called it a crash pad. Azrael owned several spread out all over the united states and Europe. He even had one in Canada, and two in Australia as well.

He was vastly wealthy, it seemed. But with the advantage of a thousand years, I supposed anyone with that sort of time on their hands could be rich if they had half a brain.

"Ow," I muttered, sucking air into my mouth around a pile of piping hot pork as it burned my tongue.

Frost crossed his mammoth arms over his chest and shook his head. "Still as impatient as ever," he said in a tone I now recognized to be his playful one even though he tried to sound authoritative and brusque.

"I can't live off one meal a day," I said after I finished chewing, exasperated. I'd been eating *maybe* once a day for a while now. With us being so busy out hunting for new recruits, and my need to sleep at least five hours a night to have any energy, there just wasn't time.

"I'm pretty sure I'm losing weight," I told him, lifting

the hem of my shirt to pull on the waistband of my leather pants. It came away from my skin, leaving a huge gap where there used to be none. "Look."

Frost's face darkened and paled all at the same time. I saw a vein in his neck thicken and his face puffed with redness. "Why the hell didn't you say anything," he growled, storming into the kitchen to wrench open the fridge and yank out a carton of eggs and small brick of cheese. He muttered something under his breath, but I didn't catch it.

"Move," he ordered, pulling a frying pan out of the cupboard where I'd just been standing. He slammed it onto the two-burner stove and lit the coil, still muttering to himself.

"Frost," I said plaintively, grabbing my plate of bacon before he could move into position in front of the stove and block me from it. "I'm good with this. It's like half a pound of meat."

He growled.

I rolled my eyes.

"You still like your cheese mixed into the egg for your omelets?"

"And—"

"Green onion," he finished for me, turning back to the fridge to pull out two stalks and set them on the cutting board on the countertop. "I remember."

I was barely able to contain a smile as warmth spread through my chest. "What?" Frost demanded, looking at me as though I'd grown two heads.

Sometimes I forgot everything they'd done for me.

Trying to prove the existence of vampires. Finding that it would never work. Becoming the monsters they sought, killing their own kind to find vengeance for me and my mother. Searching for me over a span on almost ten years. But it was hitting me now, and I stifled the urge to cry as I watched Frost whisk three eggs in a bowl with cheese and chopped green onions and pour them into a pan.

I didn't deserve them.

"Frost," I said suddenly, unable to contain the words any longer.

"Hmm?" he replied gruffly, without turning from the stove.

I swallowed. "I love you."

He stiffened, and then after a minute I saw him begin to relax as he went back to tipping the pan back and forth to spread the egg mixture over its hot surface.

He coughed a bit as though to clear something in his throat and I watched his shoulders roll back. "Yeah," he said in a low, rumbling voice. "Me too, Rosie."

I set down the piece of bacon I'd been about to stuff my face with and went into the kitchen, bear-hugging Frost from behind. He started, but then patted my hands against his wide chest and sighed. He slid the omelet off the pan and onto a plate, turning so I had to let him go. He pushed the plate into my hands and leaned down to kiss the top of my head. "Now eat," he ordered, jabbing a finger towards where I was just sitting. "All of it."

· · ·

F<small>ROST WATCHED ME EAT EVERY LAST MORSEL OF THE MEAL.</small>
He only started a conversation with me once I was
completely finished. I half expected him to order I lick the
plate clean, but I was glad he didn't.

We talked for nearly an hour before Blake came out of
the bedroom, all sleep-eyed and soft edges. A vast difference from his usual put-together self. I loved seeing him
like that. The sleepy minx in my belly purred awake at the
sight of him, wanting to pounce the moment I fixated on
the low hang of his boxer shorts and the dip of the V-
shape disappearing beneath the waistband.

Good god.

He stretched out his back and cracked his neck,
putting every muscle in his stomach, chest, and arms on
display for me to drool over. Frost, maybe sensing my
sudden arousal, nudged his head in Blake's direction.
"Fucking gorgeous, isn't he?" He said, his throaty voice
taunting.

I nodded.

Blake looked at the pair of us sitting on opposite sides
if the skinny bar-top in the kitchen. "Thanks?" he said,
yawning sleepily as he made his way into the kitchen to
guzzle a glass of water. More of a habit than anything. All
the guys still drank water and whiskey as well as blood,
but I'd never seen Azrael drink water, so I had to assume
they were in the minority.

Blake's eyes roved over me as he set his glass down, the
sleepy fog in his eyes slowly lifting. He cocked his head
and licked his lips as his eyes found my nipples beneath
the skin-tight tank top I had on.

"She eat yet?" Blake asked Frost, who nodded.

I shuddered at the way he was looking at me, my body coming alive under the force of his stare.

I knew that look. And if the gleam in his black eyes wasn't proof enough, the growing bulge of his cock beneath his gym shorts *definitely* was.

My throat went dry and my pulse immediately responded, thighs squeezing together as I licked my lips. "We can't do this here," I said with a gulp, gaze flitting to the closed door across the room where Azrael was—only ten feet away. "Az—"

"Isn't here," Frost corrected in his gruff voice, pushing off from the counter to his full height with a wicked smirk.

My brows lowered and I stifled a whimper as my belly did a little flip low and hard, an ache spreading down through my pussy.

"He isn't?" I breathed. "Where did he—"

"To check on the vamps," Blake said at the same time Frost growled, "Does it matter?"

They shared a look and I watched Frost forcibly shake off his distaste for the ancient vampire, turning his haughty stare and his focus back to me.

"Wh-when will he be back?" I stammered as Blake and Frost drew nearly, prowling like panthers about to strike. A shiver scratched up my arms and down my legs, making my back arch as I stood to back away from them, hands up in a playful gesture.

"Not for a while," Blake smirked.

I wanted to ask how long was a while exactly, but Blake lunged for me and I twirled away, shrieking with delight when I was faster than him. He chuckled as I placed myself behind the low sofa in the sitting area.

Frost's gaze narrowed on me and a glimmer of mischief crossed his jade green eyes. "You don't have far to run, Rosie," he said triumphantly, waving an arm about the small studio-sized apartment.

"Doesn't mean I'll make it easy," I purred and dodged an advance by Frost, almost knocking over a small metal side table.

I grinned, pulse pounding with the thrill of being chased. *Oh, I* liked *this.*

By the looks on their faces, they liked it, too.

Blake's fangs slid low over his bottom lip as he side-stepped closer to me, his body coiled for the spring. "Hasn't anyone ever told you it's dangerous to play games with monsters?"

Their animalistic sides were coming through from within. I could see it in the animal glare in their eyes. In their fangs, shining white against pink lips pulled back in feral growls.

I realized, as vampires, they were more in tune with their primal instinct than I could ever hope to under-stand. Most vamps, as a race, were ruled by their emotions. My raw, animalistic desires. They couldn't resist the hunt.

It added another layer to the fun game I'd set into motion. What would they do once they caught me? A small sliver of fear nudged at my breastbone and I yipped as I crouched to roll away from Frost's arm as he shot it out to grab me.

Fuck, he was fast.

"Since when have I shied away from a little danger?" I said in my best teasing voice, letting the deeper tones of my lust creep into the words. My breasts were hard beneath my shirt and there was already a slick wetness spreading between my thighs.

They could sense it.

I could see it in their eyes.

"Come on boys," I teased, muscles flexing, reflexes waiting to engage. "Come and get me."

Blake and Frost shared a look I couldn't read. Blake nodded.

What?

Blake lunged for me and I spun away, but Frost was there, too, sandwiching me between them, giving me almost no opportunity for escape. I could make a break for the bedroom, but Blake was in the way and I doubted I could get past him.

I wrinkled my nose at them, pulling my lower lip between my teeth.

I took two running steps and moved my body to slide beneath Blake's legs, my heart in my throat and my belly feeling like I just went over the top of a rollercoaster, g-force twisting my gut.

Strong hands caught me before I could even make the slide, lifting me up by the waist to heft me over a broad shoulder. Blake had lifted me over Frost's shoulder and now the big oaf's massive arm had me secured tightly there, with my head hanging down his back and my hair brushing against the ass of his jeans.

The two chuckled in triumph and before I knew it, we were back in the darkened bedroom that smelled of the vanilla musk candle we'd burned before falling asleep the night before, musty carpet, and...of *us*.

My back landed *hard* against the bed, and before I could recover, there was a weight on my hips and two hands like manacles around my wrists.

I wriggled under Blake, but it was no use.

"Take off her clothes," Blake seethed, his breaths sawing in and out through mostly clenched teeth. His fangs caught the low light coming in from the open door.

Frost ripped off my pants in the blink of an eye and I whimpered, that burning need to be touched coiling up through my womb. Next went my shirt, torn straight down the middle. I wanted them so bad, I didn't have it in me to be pissed that they'd ruined yet *another* of my shirts. I'd compel myself a whole slew of new ones the first chance I got.

I shuddered as the cool air brushed over my nipple, hardening them to stiff peaks. I pressed my hips upward, pressing my panty covered pussy against Blake's thin gym shorts.

Hi hands tightened on my wrists and he hissed, his mouth diving for my throat. I gasped as his teeth punctured my flesh, sending pain and pleasure racing through my body like an electrical current. I cried out in sweet, beautiful anguish as the venom spread, fogging my mind into a daze.

Large fingers crawled up my calves to circle my thighs and Frost's fangs came down on the thick vein just inches away from my aching pussy.

"Fuck!" I shouted into the dark, my body convulsing from the venom and the heat and the *insane* amount of pure, unfiltered *need* drowning out any other logical thought in my mind.

Blake's fangs slid free of my neck and he licked the small smear of crimson from his lower lips. His dark eyes were hazy as he beheld me through the haze of his bloodlust.

"Fuck me," I said in a broken whimper, Frost still sending shivers all over my body with each soft suckle at my thigh. "I want you both to fuck me. *Now.*"

My pussy clenched and my face twisted as Frost slid his fangs free, leaving me momentarily bereft and cold.

"Oh, I intend to," Blake said in a throaty groan, leaning down to whisper along my jaw. "But you're going to beg for it." He moved my wrists together so he could hold them both with one hand and brushed against his free one against my wet clit and snatched away my panties.

I shuddered at the sensation, dizzy with the aftereffects of the venom and need to be touched.

"Please," I whispered, ready to beg already. He didn't have to make me beg. I'd get on my knees right there and now if he would just fuck me already.

Frost slid his hand higher up my thigh, pressing his fingers gingerly against my opening. I fought against

Blake's grasp to press into his fingers, urging him to touch me deeper. More.

Harder.

But Blake held me firmly in place as Frost ran his fingers slowly back and forth over my throbbing clit, making my body shudder and jolt.

Blake maneuvered himself out of Frost's way and dipped his head over my chest, pulling my left nipple into his warm mouth. I bucked against him and his tongue pressed flat against it, circling the outer ring of hard pink flesh.

"That's it," he murmured, pulling away only to suck my other nipple into his mouth with a little *pop*.

I gasped, hips grinding against Frost's fingers now as I felt the beginning of an orgasm forming. The fuse lit.

"I'm going to take her," I heard the break in Blake's voice as he began to lose his own sense of control.

Frost grunted his approval.

"No," I managed between fevered breaths.

"I want both of you."

There was a pause and I almost cried out at the lack of sensation as their fingers and tongues froze.

I *ached* for the sensation of two cocks inside of me again. Ever since they'd done it the first time, I'd been hungry to feel that again. The pulling. The ache. The delirium of the dual sensation as two hard cocks drove into me at once.

There was another heartbeat of silence before Blake hissed. "Take her." Another pause. "There. Do it there."

My body was lifted and a wave of vertigo made dark

spots curl around the edges of my vision, as though I was on some serious drugs.

Frost carried me over to a tall ledge that rested just below a window that was entirely covered in dark paint. The ledge was thin, but it was enough for him to sit back the couple of inches he would need to angle his cock into my pussy.

He didn't wait for Blake. I could feel the strain of his muscle and the heat of his skin against my back as he tried to maintain control. But he couldn't. The moment he was in position his hands that had me lifted from the ground around my waist, pulled me down against him, shoving his cock good and hard into my pussy.

My fingernails dug into the muscle of his thighs as I groaned, adjusting to his length and girth with a massive shudder of pleasure.

As my eyes slitted open, I saw Blake, gloriously naked and covered in beautiful, intricate picture sand whorls of black in. With his eyes sparking in the dark, he could have been the devil himself.

And I'd never wanted him more.

I spread my legs as Frost adjusted his position, hammering himself into me in one good hard thrust, his hands on my hips digging in so hard I thought he might leave bruises.

I'd have to make sure they healed before he could see them.

He wouldn't like that.

Blake licked his lips as he approached. I itched to move

against Frost's cock inside of me, but I waited, wanting to feel the both of them.

Blake's dark hair fell forward to cover his eyes and I admired the hard plains of his chest as his hands circled my thighs, moving between my legs so his knees were pressed up against Frost's.

"Lean back a little more brother," Blake said, his voice deep and strained with need.

Frost did as he asked, grinding me against his hilt into position and tilting me back against him so Blake could get access from the front.

He pressed the tip of his cock against my opening, brushing it along the top part of Frosts, eliciting a shudder from the giant holding me in place.

I moaned loudly as Blake used his hand to force the head all the way in. The pressure of him in there with Frost made my head fall back in ecstasy.

"Yeah," I ground out. "Just like that."

As Blake began to move, I pulled myself back up, wanting to look him in the eyes as he fucked me.

Frost nuzzled against my neck, kissing the still healing flesh around Blake's bite mark, lapping gently against the still wet blood running down to my collarbone.

Blake pumped into me, his fangs out again, bared as his eyes bored into me.

His thrusts became harder, more violent, rocking me back and forth harder and faster against Frost's cock.

I felt Frost's body as it began to harden and shudder beneath me.

My own orgasm was rushing to the surface and I

moaned wildly and shouted, nails holding tight to hard muscle and sinew like a vise.

Blake growled as he fucked me and just when I thought I was about to cleave in two, Frost shuddered against my back and Blake came into me, sending me headlong into a long orgasm that had me letting go of Frost to cling to Blake, burying my face into his sweat-slicked chest to stifle the sounds of my screams.

CHAPTER 14

"*T*his nest is the one that most likely is already under my brother's control," Azrael said as we parked the rented car in a quiet lot behind a bank of tall shopping buildings.

We walked briskly down an alley between two buildings and turned left, Frost, Blake, and I followed Azrael's lead as usual.

"Too bad," I said, not at all unphased. Last night had been almost boring. I was itching for some action and couldn't wait to get my hands dirty.

"Easy tiger," Blake purred.

I winked at him.

We walked for a few blocks until coming upon an older apartment complex made up of three buildings. It was clear right away which one belonged to the vampire nest. It was smaller than the other two—only about six or seven floors. And it was covered in graffiti. The brick façade crumbling and in disrepair. Judging by the feeling of *otherness* radiating out from it, the vamps had the whole place to themselves.

Azrael paused on the sidewalk, just outside of the light of the earnest flickering streetlamp. He held his hand out to us. "Wait," he said, and we stopped behind him.

"What is it?" Frost asked gruffly, his face pinching.

Azrael shushed him forcefully and tipped his head toward the building, listening. I was about ready to start tapping my foot when his lips parted in surprise and he dug into the pocket of his jeans for the car keys. He tossed them to me, and I snatched them out of the air, cocking my head at him.

"They know you're here," he said in a low, dangerous tone, glaring at the building.

My eyes narrowed. "How?"

He shrugged. "Maybe one of the other nests figured out who you were and spread the word. I'm not sure. But they know you're in Phoenix. They know you might be coming."

I shrugged. "So what?"

Azrael glared at me.

"Either they're on our side or not. If the former, great. If the latter, you might need some help cleaning house."

Azrael ran a hand over his face and his chest expanded with a heavy intake of breath. "There are too many."

I scoffed and walked past him, heading for the building. Shockingly, he let me pass. In fact, he let me get all the way to the edge of the street before I stopped of my own volition.

That feeling of otherness had already been strong, but

with each step I'd taken toward the ramshackle apartment building, it'd grown stronger. The vampire nest didn't just control the whole building. If the feeling in my gut was right, it was also filled to the tits with them.

The omnipresent feeling was like a buzzing in my blood. Like a thousand tiny insects crawling over my skin.

Ugh.

I turned around and came back, trying not to let it show that I was put off. But if Azrael was in my head like he always was, he would already know. "All the more reason for me to come," I told him. "Looks like you'll need my help."

He frowned. "No. Not this time."

There was no space for argument in his tone, and despite the warm balm of the Phoenix night, I shivered with barely contained rage.

"If I'm not going, then *they're* not going, either," I said defiantly, jabbing my fingers toward Blake and Frost.

"Rosie," Frost started, but I cut him a look and he groaned, falling silent.

The crease in Azrael's brow softened, and when he spoke again it was with the patronizing tone of an elder scolding a child. "If you stay away," he explained. "We'll have a better shot of converting them to our side. They want you dead, Rose. It appears the bounty on your head has doubled..."

Great.

"If you aren't there, there's a better chance that there will be no blood shed. They will either agree to side with us, or they will deny the offer."

"What's the point if they'll just try to kill me once they find out I'm with you?"

Azrael shook his head. "They won't. Not once they know what you can give them."

"So, basically, you're going to trick them into siding with you by not mentioning me, and then lift the wool from their eyes only *after* you've snared them with a taste of sunlight?"

Azrael's face hardened. "Yes."

I tipped my head back and forth. It wasn't a bad plan. "I say we just skip this one," I said after a minute. "There are other nests. *Tons*. If you think it's too dangerous for me to go with you guys, let's just go to the next."

Blake and Frost muttered between themselves. It seemed Frost agreed with me, but Blake was undecided.

"It's a large nest," Azrael continued. "And from what I can hear at this distance, Rafe hasn't approached them yet. There are at least forty in there. That is a big portion of the force we will need to take him down."

I grit my teeth.

"Forty?" Blake asked incredulously. "Are you sure? I've never heard of a nest so big."

Azrael nodded. "Yes, I'm certain."

"Rose," Blake said, tugging me by the arm to face him. "If we can convert them, that's *huge*. Think about it. *Forty*."

"And if you can't?" I insisted, my jaw still taut as a chill ran up my spine. "If they attack?"

Blake didn't have a reply. At least, not one that would convince me to let them go without me.

"You promised Ethan," Azrael said, breaking the tepid silence.

"What?" I hissed, turning on him as I yanked my arm free from Blake.

He looked down at me with an apology in his gaze. "You promised Ethan you wouldn't put yourself in any unnecessary danger. You promised him that you would be careful."

"Fucking bastard," I growled, balling my hands. I *had* promised Ethan that. "But that doesn't fucking mean I'm going to let *them* go in there with you."

Azrael glanced from me to the guys at my back. "Would you prefer to wait in the car with Rose?" he asked them.

"Fuck no," Blake replied, his body tensing in anticipation. A smirk curling up one side of his lips.

"I don't—" Frost began in his damage-control voice, as though ready to lay down the law.

But Azrael interrupted him, his hand reaching out to turn my gaze back to him. I shied away from his touch, shivering. He dropped his hand and swallowed. "If any vampire in that building gets it in their head to attack, I will know it, and I *will* get them out. I can't compel so many at once, but they would do anything to protect their queen. All I would have to do is compel a few to kill her, and they would have their hands full. You have my word; no harm will come to them." Azrael pushed a stray hair back from his face, and I found a sincerity in his gaze that I hadn't seen there before. He really meant it.

"I'll need their testimony to help convince the nest to join us, or else I would go alone."

I groaned. "*Ugh.* Fine. You want to go without me?" I whirled on Frost and Blake. "*Go* then. I'll just go wait in the goddamned car like a good little Rose."

I didn't wait for them to reply before I stormed back in the direction we'd come from. "If either of you comes back with so much as a fucking *scratch*, I'm withholding sex for a month," I called back over my shoulder, fuming.

I briefly considered ducking into the pub I could hear blaring alternative rock down the road but thought better of it. Two fingers of whiskey weren't worth facing the wrath of Azrael and my guys if they somehow returned to the rental car before I did.

Shoulders hitched with frustration, I stalked down the alleyway, muttering to myself the whole way. I *hated* that they were going in without me. And if I was being honest with myself, it wasn't *only* because I wouldn't be there to protect them—I trusted Azrael. Shocking, but it was true.

No, it was that *I* wanted to blow off some steam, too. I wanted to stake a few bloodsuckers and live off the beautiful high of adrenaline and laser-sharp senses. Just for a minute.

I was fucking *bored.*

I'd killed more vampires in a single weekend than I had in the few weeks since Azrael captured me. I wasn't used to all this…all this…*not* killing shit.

The darkness inside me was starting to spread now that I wasn't feeding it to keep it at bay. More flashbacks of mom were hitting me than they had in years. More burning hatred. *More* blind frustration.

If I didn't have my guys to distract me and keep me sane, I had to wonder if I'd have fully flown off the hinges by now.

I looked up from kicking at tiny stones in the alley and froze. There wasn't anything there, but there was this sensation I couldn't place. It was like a rodent skittering down my back. It was a suffocating weight on my chest. Like the alley was suddenly clogged with energy.

An acrid smell wrinkled my nose, like hot, burning metal.

I recognized it a heartbeat later. It was the smell that accompanied Amala's spell when she'd healed me.

It was the scent of magic.

But I put it together too late as the portal opened up on the wall next to where I stood. Opening the pock-marked cement with a charged ring of (color) to reveal a gaping hole that made my heart plummet and all the blood drain from my face. Like standing too close to a passing train, the sense of vertigo washed over me and I stumbled, trying to keep my footing as shapes appeared in the dark.

A mass of moving black that emerged into the dim lighting of the Phoenix alleyway and was revealed as a group of vampires dressed in dark colors. Their fangs glinting in the moonlight. Their eyes glaring with malice and amusement at my shock.

I drew my stakes and slid my right foot back, baring my own teeth as they circled me. They were all big. All of them exuded that aura of age that only came with a long-changed vampire. My flesh broke out in goosebumps as the combined sensation of otherness doused me. I was outmatched. That much was clear.

But it didn't mean I was about to go down without a damned good fight. Judging the distance between where I was in the alley and where the guys and Frost were a few blocks away at the apartment complex, I thought I had about a fifty-fifty chance of Azrael being able to hear me.

It was worth a shot.

I kicked out as one stepped in too close, getting him good in the gut with the heel of my boot as I whirled and jabbed the blunt end of my stake into the jaw of the one behind me as he lunged in, arms outstretched to grab me.

"Azrael!" I bellowed, ducking low to kick out the feet of the one on the left, my heart thrumming behind my ribcage. I rose and swung my arm back, wincing as my knuckled crashed against bone and blood sprayed over my fingertips.

From the corner of my eye, I saw a flash of orange light in the dark abyss where there used to be a wall. It expanded and burst just as I finished driving my stake into the one with the broken nose. The magic hit me like a fucking freight train.

I jarred from the force of impact and my hands were sucked behind my back as though by some cosmic vacuum. They bound themselves together and I gasped, trying to get them apart to no avail.

I couldn't move them, and I was damn near about to dislodge my shoulder trying. "The fuck?" I cursed under my breath just as I looked up and saw the slitted eyes of Amala as she emerged from the black.

"That's about enough," she said in her strange accent, eyeing me as though I was goods to be appraised. She seemed pleased with what she found.

"Amala?" I asked, incredulous. My mind had only just begun to recognize the betrayal it was witnessing when a hard *knock* on the back of my head made my vision waver and then darken as my body flew forward into the witch's portal.

CHAPTER 15

I came to sandwiched between two burly vampires, in a congested elevator on its way up a shaft. My stomach lurched at the dizzying sensation and my sides squeezed inward painfully as I bent my head to wretch all over vamp number one's shoes.

"Ugh," he groaned in disgust. "Fucking bitch just puked all over my shoes."

I tried to paw away the foul-tasting ichor from my lips, but my hands felt numb and detached.

My body was shuffled away from vamp number one and the other one wrapped an arm like an iron bar around my middle, securing me to him. I was still coming to, finding my strength. Waiting impatiently for all the information tunnels in my body to reconnect so I could kill them both.

They were old. Strong. That much was apparent the moment I regained consciousness, but I'd taken on worse.

I just needed to get my head straight and then…

The doors dinged open and the vampire with his arm around my middle dragged me from the elevator and into a wide space. I inhaled deeply, the weight of the suffocating chamber of the elevator blissfully lifted.

The vamp with the vomit coated shoes took off to the left to go behind a tall bar where there was a sink and washcloths among a fully-stocked wall of liquor backlit in shades of blue and yellow. My vision swam and the colors all melded together into a shade of teal.

In front of the bar and stretching in front of the elevator was a large living space. A living room with leather sofas and a rug that looked like it was made from the fur of a massive wolf was at its center.

Beyond that was a wide circular balcony, sealed off with French doors, but beyond them I could see the night sky.

A way out.

A spike of adrenaline kickstarted my heart and lit my neural pathways ablaze in startling clarity. The blur in my vision began to abate. My fingers twitched to attack, but I reined myself in, waiting for the right moment. With a sly feel of my inner thighs, I found that my stakes had been removed.

The press of my katana across my back was no longer there, either.

Fuck.

But low, in the side of my boot, was a small dagger. And in my hair were two silver chopsticks I could still feel securing the dark strands into a now-loose bun.

It would have to do.

The vamp by the sink returned and I forced my body to slump, groaning as though I was still completely out of it. Feigning weakness.

"I hope you cleaned up after yourself," the one holding me up barked at the other. "If Rafe finds vomit in his fucking sink, it'll be your head."

It was like he'd injected ice water into my blood.

I'd already assumed I was in Rafe's safe house, but I didn't want it to be true. Better that Amala had simply abducted me for her own ends. But no, *she* was the witch Rafe had hired. Amala, Azrael's so-called *friend,* had somehow been persuaded to join that dark side. She'd betrayed Azrael.

I shuddered to think what he'd do to her if he ever got the chance.

I shuddered even more when I realized Azrael and the guys could be looking for me right at this moment. Had they noticed I was missing? Could Azrael have heard me call out to him from that alley several blocks away? Had they even gotten out of that vampire infested apartment building alive?

I squeezed my eyes shut and forced my mind to concentrate. Cooperate. I could be worried about them right now. I had to worry about me. Fix the biggest problem first—then worry about all the other ones. I swallowed to wet my parched throat and let the anxious thoughts fade into background noise, allowing me to sharpen my focus.

The second vamp grabbed a set of keys out of his

pocket as he neared. "Come on," he said to the other. "Let's lock her up before he gets back."

My heart pumped harder in my chest, the adrenaline a wild animal in my veins now.

"I think she's coming to—"

I swung my hand up and twisted in his grasp, tearing a sharp-pointed chopstick from my hair to jab deep into his ocular cavity. He released me instantly and fell, a hand to his face, clutching his destroyed eye.

The other was on top of me before I was ready, knocking me hard to the ground. The air left my lungs in a painful *whoosh* and it took all I had to get some air back in and stop the vampire from connecting a blow that surely would have rendered me unconscious.

Not today, Satan.

I kicked my knee up from the floor and nailed him good and hard in the balls. The instant of surprise was all I needed to buck him off, draw the dagger from my boot and ram it down into his chest cavity. But the sucker was fast. His hands gripped mine, stopping the blade a mere inch from its intended target.

I grunted with the effort of pushing it down into his heart, but it was no use and I knew it. He was stronger.

I shouted an ear-slitting battle cry, using every muscle I had. "Die," I managed between clenched teeth. "Fucker."

The other vampire had dislodged the chopstick from his skull and was healing rapidly. Soon there would be two to contend with. I needed to do something. I needed to—

"Well this is interesting," a satin smooth voice spoke

from the open elevator doors, the ominous ding of its arrival still echoing around Raphael as he stepped out of the lift.

The vampire beneath me gasped and I used his surprise at seeing his master there, looking down on him with disdain to press the blade the rest of the way down into the dense muscle of his heart. He jerked under me and then grew still, his final breath leaving his lips in a cloud of rank metallic breath.

I choked and rolled off him to lay flat on my back, breathless with my shoulders aching from the tremendous effort of fighting back against the vamp's immortal strength.

It was no use now, anyway. I was done. I couldn't beat Raphael. And the other one wouldn't dare attack unless ordered now. Rafe clearly wanted me alive or Tweedle-dee and Tweedle-dumb would have killed me while I was knocked out.

Raphael went to the vampire, staring in horror down at his deceased friend. "Rod?" the vamp said in a watery voice, staring down at the corpse with a sort of reverence only reserved for lovers.

"Don't worry," Rafe said, floating over to the vampire with a ring of still-wet blood dripping from his now healed eye socket. "You've just now proven your complete incompetence." The other vampire seemed as though he was in shock, he couldn't stop staring wide-eyed and slack-jawed at his lover.

Poor fucker had no idea what was about to happen. But I did.

Rafe placed a consoling hand on the vamp's shoulder, pouting down at the blood pooling around his lackey. "That's going to stain my floor," he mused, a crease forming between his brows. A flicker of rage coming to life in his mismatched eyes.

My throat tightened.

Now.

I jumped to my feet and ran. Not looking back for a second. I leaped over the back of the sofa, jumped up a step I hadn't seen in the floor, and threw my body toward the glass pane on the left French door leading out to the balcony. Elbows out to break the glass and protect my face.

I bounced back like a fucking tennis ball off a wall. My elbows felt like they'd been shattered, and the jagged pain of a thousand needles radiated up and down my arms, from fingertips to shoulders. I sucked in a breath through bared teeth and clenched my hands, curling inward on myself against the wolf's fur rug.

A slow clap pierced the air and I looked up, heaving, at where Raphael was standing over two corpses. One of them missing a head.

"Thought you were worried about staining your floor," I muttered, the words bent and broken from trying to force them out through the raw agony in the bones of my elbows. I was starting to worry I'd actually fractured them.

Fucking hell.

It would take at least an hour for that shit to heal.

"A bit late for that, I think," he said with a sly grin and glittering eyes.

Oh good, I'm amusing him.

Rafe walked over to a panel in the wall next to the elevator and pressed a small square button, speaking into the intercom. "Clean up in the penthouse," he said in a lighthearted tone, not unlike one you might hear in the aisles of a supermarket.

While he was distracted, I used all the gas I had left in the tank to push myself up and make another run for the door, this time forcing my elbow to bend enough so I could unlatch and open it with the handle.

My hand had only just closed around the shining brass knob when hard, icy fingers dug into the bone of my right shoulder and ripped me backward, sending me sprawling back onto the rug in a heap.

My head knocked against the marble edge of a small side table and a guttural sound reverberated out from my chest. I cursed, clutching the throbbing corner of my skull as stars flashed in my vision.

"Oh, I'm sorry, did that hurt?"

When I blinked again, Raphael was there, his face inches from my own, grinning wickedly. This close up, it was so easy to tell he wasn't his brother. But if you didn't know them, it would be almost impossible. The same hair, though Rafe's was several inches short. The same unsettling eyes. Sharp cheekbones and large, muscled frame. Though I thought Azrael was bigger.

A flash of white and my head snapped back. I tasted blood on my tongue and a sting in my cheek.

"Don't *ever* compare me to *him*. He is weak. *Pathetic*. I should have killed him in the womb."

I shook my head to clear it of the daze he's put there and licked the blood from my lip.

Raphael pulled my hand away from my head and held it tightly in his. I looked down, horrified, but completely unable to move it. He was examining it as though it was the most interesting thing he'd seen all day. Then he brought forward the stump of his hand to compare.

I stopped breathing.

I'd almost forgotten I'd taken the bastard's hand. I'd half expected it to grow back.

"I should take yours," he mused, turning my hand this way and that in his clammy grip. "Tit for tat and all that."

I braced myself, waiting for him to literally rip the appendage from my body, but he didn't.

Instead, he began to laugh and released my hand. I pulled it into my chest, clutching it to me in relief that I still had it.

"Oh, my love…I intend to take *much* more from you than that."

The way he said it made my body chill. I was taking tiny sips of air, unable to get more than that into my lungs under the weight of what he was implying.

"What am I doing here?" I asked him plainly.

He didn't respond, just rocked back on his heels and cocked his head at me. "You're a pretty thing, aren't you?"

His gaze fell onto my lips and I resisted the urge to vomit again at the stark memory of the way he'd forced his mouth onto me once before.

Raphael pushed the russet hair from his face and smirked. "That will make it much easier."

Confused, my brows furrowed. "Make *what* easier?"

Just then the elevator door slid open and a group of three vampires stepped into the penthouse. They paused upon seeing their fallen comrades, faces blanching. But other than the paling of their features, none objected to the scene before them. They barely flinched.

"Clean it up," Raphael ordered them without giving any explanation then he turned back to me.

His eyes bored into mine and I realized what he was about to do a second before it was too late. "Come," he commanded, the force of his compulsion washing over me like a motherfucking tidal wave. I grimaced and tried to stop my body from responding, but I couldn't.

When Rafe held out his still-attached hand to me, I took it. And when he helped me to stand, I shouted a string of profanity at him, but could do little more than speak. I had lost all control of everything else. My body thrummed with only the need to *come with Raphael* as he led us away out of the living space and through a side door I hadn't noticed before, hidden behind a column.

He walked me along, cursing and griping the whole way, shaking as I waged an internal war, trying to deny his order.

It was like trying to move a thousand-pound block of cement while suffocating under water. My face was probably all shades of purple and red from the effort.

"Oh, give it up," he said, interrupting my grunted death

threats and curses. "It's no use and you know it. You'll only cause yourself an aneurism."

"Fucking dick."

"Here we are," he said with a wide grin that I was starting to realize meant he was about to do or say something particularly nasty.

We had stopped after walked through stark white corridors for a while at a plain metal door. There were no windows anywhere. Just white walls. White ceilings. White linoleum floors scuffed with little streaks of black here and there.

He peered down at me, eyes alight. "It's time for you to meet my other treasures."

He swung the door open and I heard the low murmur of voices emanating from within the dimly lit space beyond. A scent like soft vanilla threaded through with the distinct aroma of jasmine filled my nose.

"Come," Rafe ordered again and my feet began to move of their own accord, following close on his heels as we moved inside and the heavy door clicked shut behind us, sealing us inside.

They emerged from all different directions like spirits from the shadows. *Buck naked.* Eight of them. Eight naked women came forward with gazes filled with reverent adoration. Smiles bloomed over their faces as they saw him. I cringed.

"Oh, my love," A particularly beautiful African American woman said as she stepped into his side, wrapping an arm around him as she pressed her breasts against his chest and tipped her head up for a kiss. Her plump lips brushed his and he reached around her to grab a handful of her round ass. "Gloria," he murmured, gesturing to me at his side as the others gathered around, all of them finding a part of him to touch. All of them shuddering as they did, as though the mere feel of him was a balm to them. A fix.

He was their drug and they were drinking him in.

My stomach roiled. They were...human.

Not all of them. But seven of the eight were. And if I wasn't mistaken, the one who was not fully human was not fully vampire, either. She'd been recently turned and hadn't completed her transformation.

"This is Rose," Raphael said, meeting each of their gazes.

"Sister," one of the girls whispered. She shouldn't have been more than eighteen. My lungs constricted.

I shook my head at her.

"Wife," another said in a dreamy tone, as though her consciousness was *very* far away.

He'd compelled them all, I realized. They were all under his spell. At his beck and call. Would respond to his every whim and desire. It was the most disgusting thing I'd ever seen.

"Yes," Raphael told the one who'd called me *wife*. "Yes, she is."

CHAPTER 16

I couldn't leave the room. Every time I got even remotely close to the door, this awful searing pain radiated up through my heels all the way to the precipice of my skull. It was utterly crippling and would only abate if I stepped away.

It was the way Raphael had made it. It was how he made them all stay in this room. By compelling them not to be able to leave. But he didn't stop there. He made even attempting it painful. All he had to do was tell me I couldn't leave, and it would be excruciating if I tried.

I pulled at my hair and growled in frustration, backing away from the metal door for the eighteenth time since he'd left me in the large, plush living quarters with his *wives*.

The walls were painted in dark hues, draped with heavy curtains, low lit sconces spaced evenly throughout the section of building. There were no windows that I could see. So that ruled jumping out of one and hoping to survive the fall out of the question.

There was soft furniture all around. Beds and divans. Sofas and massive cushions littered the area and stretched far back into the space. It was massive.

"Here," said a sweet one called Penny. She had blonde hair and blue eyes and not an ounce of fat on her. The epitome of what I imaged when thinking of spring break. She held out a glass of water to me. "You should have some water. Husband likes us to stay hydrated."

Ignoring the last bit, I took the glass and downed it. Regardless of what fucking *husband* said, I was thirsty.

"He likes us..." she hesitated, her eyes flickering over my bloodied leathers and matted hair. "...clean, too. Maybe you would like a bath? We have a lovely bath with jasmine and rose petals and—"

"Penny, right?"

She nodded enthusiastically.

"Your husband is a fucking rapist."

Her blue eyes widened.

"Oh no," she said, staring at me earnestly now. Her already high voice rising even more in pitch. "He would never do anything so horrible. He *loves* us. He is so kind."

The woman Rafe had called Gloria earlier kneeled next to us and folded her hands in her lap, the picture of elegance. This close up, in the brighter lighting, she almost took my breath away. I wasn't sure I'd ever seen anyone so utterly *perfect*.

Perfect tits. A trim waist. An ass to kill for—and that was saying something since I was rather fond of my own

—and a face without flaw. Wide deep brown eyes. Skin like darkest onyx. Hair a rich ebony in a wild mane around her face.

"Husband is a marvelous lover," she said in a deep, haunting tone. She reached out and brushed my hair back from my face. "He will please you."

Oh, *hell* no.

I sprang to my feet and made a run for the door, thinking if maybe I just moved fast enough, without thinking about it, that I could break through the solid wall of compulsion keeping me inside.

I made it four feet before the pain exploded in my skull and I retreated, whimpering on my hands and knees against the plush carpet.

"You must stop," another of the wives said, coming to stand with the other two. This one was Latin American. If the deep golden hue of her skin and waving brown hair wasn't enough of a clue, her accent was thick and heavy with Spanish influence. "You will hurt yourself."

Together they were a rainbow of color. Their eyes, though glassy with the haze of compulsion, were also filled with genuine worry for Rafe's new *pet*.

The Latin American one, the oldest of the three, stood, and I noticed the silky skin of a c-section scar on her lower abdomen. Did they have families? Children? Husbands? Friends?

Who was missing them?

A renewed fury pulsed through me.

I *was* going to get out of there. And I was taking these women with me.

CHAPTER 17

*S*etting aside my pride, I did eventually accept the offered bath, if only to wash away the crusty itch of dried blood on my skin and the grease from my hair.

It was near impossible to tell how long I'd been in the chambers with Raphael's wives. Without a single clock anywhere in sight and no access to natural light, it could have been a few hours, or an entire day. I couldn't be sure.

"Now, is that not better?" Luz asked, her Spanish accent making the words sound almost lyrical. She patted me on the shoulder as I stepped from the bathroom with a towel around my naked body. There was no door to the bathroom, or it seemed anywhere else in the entire chamber except the one exit and one other that was locked up tight at the very back of the space.

I had to assume that one was *not* an exit since it didn't cause me any pain to go near it. I was even able to wrap my hand around the handle and tug without a problem.

Another room, then. A locked one.

I toweled off my hair and walked alongside Luz back into the main atrium-like area. If it weren't for the fact that they were all hostages here. That Raphael was using them for blood and sex, it would be beautiful. Like what I imagined the den of a wealthy silk trader in Morocco to have as her chamber.

"Where does that door lead?" I asked Luz, pointing at a small half-door to our right that squatted a mere three feet from the ground. It looked like a door for a child and it was the only other one save for the exit.

Luz frowned. "That's where we go if we misbehave," she told me with a pained expression. "Most of the wives have never seen the inside of it."

"But you have?" I prodded.

"Just one time. It is dark and very cold. Bare. Just a box with no way out."

My brows drew down. "What did you do to upset him?"

Luz shrugged and turned, giving me a full-frontal view of her naked body. I was past the point of trying to avert my eyes every time one of them looked at me. It was so strange how comfortable they were walking around completely fucking naked.

She tilted her head, and her eyes unfocused. "I can not remember," she said in a dazed whisper.

Of course, she couldn't. He would have made her forget and told her never to do it again. I didn't miss the fact that he left with her the memory of the solitary room.

A warning to the others should they attempt to misbehave.

Sick fuck.

My gaze lowered to her c-section scar again and I swallowed hard before gesturing to it. "You have children?" I said, more of a statement than a question.

Her lips parted and for the briefest second I saw the haze lift from her eyes, but then it was falling again, shrouding her under the weight of Rafe's compulsion.

"No, of course not. Not yet," she said with a wan smile, showing off perfect white teeth that seemed almost to glow against her tan skin and lush dusty rose lips. "But I hope to be the one to give husband the child he wants."

My airway sealed off and I almost choked. "What the hell did you just say?"

Luz looked at me, puzzled. "I said that I do not have children, but—"

"No," I barked. "The other bit. The part about Raphael wanting a child? Did I fucking hear that right?"

She seemed mildly perturbed by my language but didn't comment on it. Instead she shrugged and rolled her spine back to stand a little straighter. "Yes. It is very difficult for him. He is, how you say? Infertile?"

I put a hand to my stomach to quell the nervous energy and roiling of bile there. Picturing an innocent child in the hands of a monster like Raphael was one of the most horrific images I could ever conjure, and I'd seen some fucked up shit.

"No shit. He's a vampire."

Ignoring me, she went on, "But there are cases of this

—a pregnancy—happening between a vampire and a mortal."

I'd never heard of this, and Luz, sensing my confusion, led me by the hand to a scattering of thick fluffy cushions in one unoccupied corner of the space. "It is *rare*," she explained. "But not *impossible*. A man's seed survives him, even after his heart stops."

"But not for a thousand years."

"Husband thinks he can make a child, so we help him to try. He has no family. No heir."

I shook my head vehemently. "He's not good, Luz. He can't have a child. He would only harm it."

Her eyes glazed over as though she wasn't even hearing me.

"It will be over soon, I think," she mused aloud, and her eyes cleared as she looked down at me with kind, motherly eyes. "Now we have *you*."

"Me?"

She nodded. "Yes. Husband told us he find a way for us to be a family. He only needed the help of a Rose. I thought he meant a flower. Maybe a magic one. But now I think I was wrong. I think he meant you."

Oh hell *no.*

My mind raced. Could he? Could I be impregnated by a vampire? Surely, I would have been already if it were possible, right?

Or wait, maybe his intention wasn't to rape me, but to—

I gasped, my hand flying up to cover the sound and stifle the rise of bile in my throat.

If my blood could act as temporary sunblock for a vampire. Could it also reanimate a vampire's sperm long enough for him to *become* temporarily fertile?

What would a child born of an immortal even be like? Would it just be a normal child or would be born the hell spawn of a monster, thirsty for blood instead of milk? Unnaturally strong and allergic to sunlight?

No. This could not be allowed to happen.

The immortals had laws. They had an entire witch's council who helped uphold those laws. *This,* what Rafe was doing with these women here was *definitely* fucking illegal.

And what he intended to do—to make a child from immortal seed—that had to be against some sort of law too, right?

How was he getting away with all of this?

Why was no one stopping him?

It crossed my mind that perhaps they couldn't. He may be too strong. Too well protected.

"Husband will return soon," she said after a few beats of silence. "I think he will choose you tonight."

"What?" I asked, still reeling from all this new information.

"You should make ready for him."

Heart pounding, I rose to head back in the direction of the bathroom. Everything out here was soft cushioned. If I was going to put up a fight, I'd need something to use. Something harder than my fists.

"Thank you, Luz," I told her, my heart hurting for the

life she clearly lost but could not remember. "I *will* go make ready for him."

"Bueno," she replied with a smile. "I will tell the others to leave husband for you tonight. You should have him alone your first time."

I gagged and forced my smile to remain intact until I was out of her line of sight.

IT WASN'T LONG BEFORE HE RETURNED. MAYBE AN HOUR. Maybe two.

When I heard the door click open, I stilled, rendering my mind blank, focusing only on erecting a wall of white stone around my mental barriers. There hadn't been much to use in the bathroom, but I was now the proud owner of a metal shower rod I planned to use as a bo staff and two forked wooden hair pins I found in a drawer.

I faintly heard Rafe greeting the wives again. Heard their fawning remarks on his handsomeness, on how much they missed him, on how they wished he would stay.

So messed up.

Then I heard Luz say the words, "Your Rose is ready for you," and it was like a bolt of lightning struck me all the way through, lighting my nerve endings ablaze.

My mind tried to conjure all sort of images. Him trying to get in my pants. Me ripping his balls off and stuffing them down his throat. But I squelched them in favor of white walls, blank canvas. Blank thoughts behind a blank wall.

"Is she now?" Raphael trilled, clearly amused.

Lengthening my spine, I exited the bathroom, wearing my leather pants and the tank top I had on under my usual corset-like leather top. Bare feet. Hair fixed in a loose twist at the back of my head with the forked comb. The metal rod from the shower was tucked carefully just inside the bathroom.

Blank walls.

Blank walls.

I added another brick.

Another.

Raphael gazed at me, his brows pinching slightly, his smile fading. From afar he could have been Azrael, and I shuddered at the warring feeling inside me. He was in a thin navy button-up that was buttoned down to his mid-chest, revealing skin like ivory. Flawless and rock hard with latent muscle.

His broad shoulders, sexy on Azrael, managed to only look hulking and awkward on his twin. His hair was tied back like Azrael usually wore it, too. In a low messy tie at the base of his neck, a few shorter strands dangling around his unsettling eyes.

Place another brick. Blank white walls.

Rafe's eyes traveled up and down my body and a flicker of something like approval made my insides flip. Suddenly I wished I'd left myself blood-caked and dirty, reeking of stale sweat and rusted pennies.

"Is it true?" He crooned, tilting his head to one side, watching me like a falcon circling its prey. "Have you decided to play nice, my love?"

Barf.

Tensely, I gave a single small nod, my fingers itching to ball to fists.

He clucked his tongue, stroking the blond girl, Penny's hair while another of his wives, the one called Jennifer— the one who was on her way to becoming a vampire— nibbled playfully at his left ear.

"That's really too bad," he said with an exaggerated frown. "Takes all the fun out of it, don't you think?"

He turned and the hand he had playing in Penny's blonde hair dove through the long waving strands to violently take hold of her by the back of the neck. She whimpered, but the sound quickly morphed into a length-ened moan as he stole a rough kiss from her lips.

Calm, Rose, I demanded of myself. *Stay calm.*

He pulled away and gauged my reaction, his brows furrowing again. "I see my brother has taught you how to conceal your thoughts," he said, licking his lips. "But I hope you know that all it would take is one good tap against your carefully constructed walls to make them crumble."

I gulped.

"Don't worry," he said. "It's nice not to hear the thoughts of everyone in the room. Keeps things...interesting."

I gritted my teeth, hefting brick after brick after brick into place, strengthening my barriers just in case he changed his mind. Soon the wall would be the biggest I'd ever built. Maybe it would stand up against him if he did try to tear it down.

That would teach him to stop be so fucking cocky.

"No more games," I said, my tone unwavering. "What is it you want from me, Raphael?"

"I think you know. Luz has already shared my desire with you, didn't you mi amor?"

"Si. Ella es tu Rosa, no?"

"Yes," Rafe replied to her. "She is the Rose I told you I needed."

My fingernails dig deep into my palms, steadying me. "Well, now you have me. What is it you plan to do with me?"

I wanted him to say it. If he planned to fucking *plant his seed* inside of me, I wanted to know right fucking now. I wouldn't be able to stop myself from attacking for another second if that was the case. My body tensed for his reply, blood warming in my veins.

"Several things," he said cryptically, a glimmer in his eyes. "Word has spread of an ability you possess to bestow a vampire with the ability to walk in the sun. Temporarily, from what I've heard."

I didn't dare respond.

"The rumor says that the power to do such a thing lies in your pure Vocari blood, is that true?"

My heart hammered in my chest, and I made the mistake of grazing my eyes over his for the barest instant he needed to drag the information out with his compulsion. "Is. That. True?"

"Yes," I rasped; the word forcefully expelled from my lips.

Raphael smiled. It was the creepiest thing I think I'd ever seen.

"Very good. Then that is what I need. I have no desire to walk in sunlight. Vampires are creatures of the dark—the shadows are where we belong. Where we *thrive*. No. It isn't sunlight I desire, but the other possible side-effects of such a temporary *cure*."

"Take my blood then. Get me a cup and I'll fill it for you."

It wouldn't work. My blood needed to be synthesized like in the serum Eth—I cut the thought short. I couldn't risk giving up that information. I placed another brick within my walled-off mind instead. Then another.

"I think not. I'm a vampire, Rose. A *king*. I drink only from the vein."

"Not a fucking chance."

"There will be consequences if you refuse me."

I bit my tongue. There was no way in hell I was going to *let* him bite me. But he could force me…

"I won't force you," he crooned, and I wondered if he'd somehow heard my thought just then. I rushed to brace my mental barriers. "I want you to give it to me freely. It's so much more fun that way."

Fucking bastard.

"I won't."

"As you wish." Raphael turned to Jennifer and plunged a hand into her chest. The squelch of blood and the crunch of bone shattered my resolve. Her pretty brown eyes widened, and her mouth opened in a silent scream. Raphael ripped her heart from her chest cavity, and she slumped to the plush carpet at his feet, crimson pooling rapidly around her prone form.

Penny screamed blood murder. Luz was on her knees, hands fluttering over Jennifer as though the young girl had been her own daughter.

"No, no, no, no," Luz was saying over and over.

Hot rage boiled up within me.

The other girls began to sob and whimper and shout.

Raphael took a long breath in through his nostrils and rolled his shoulders back, a look of pure bliss contorting his features. "Fear," he said with eyes alight. "My favorite scent."

I swallowed back bile.

"Porque?" Luz asked, tears streaming freely now.

Raphael smiled down at her and then looked to the others as each of them looked to him for an explanation. "Forget this," he said in a deadpan voice and the sobs and whimpering began to subside. They all stilled as he lifted Jennifer's body from the carpet and walked back toward the front door. He opened it and tossed her unceremoniously out into the hall, chucking her heart out after her.

Then he waltzed back in, wiping his hand on his jeans. "Now," he continued as he approached his eight wives all still waiting in a daze around the bloodstained carpet. "There was no Jennifer. You will forget her. She never existed."

They nodded along with his compulsion.

"Oh dear," he continued after a pause. "It seems I've spilled some wine. Would you ladies mind cleaning it up for your husband?"

And just like that they were back to smiles and complacence.

"You're the worst sort of monster," I muttered, watching as the *seven* wives rushed around to gather cloths and a bowl of water from the bathroom, completely unaware of the horror they'd just witnessed.

Once they were all busy, Raphael strode over the patch of crimson and came closer to me. He looked between the women who were all scrubbing at the red stains without a care in the world. Penny even giggled a bit at something Grace had said.

My heart ached for them.

"Now," Raphael said. "Would you permit me a taste, or shall I rid myself of another wife? Jennifer was useless to me having already begun the change. But the others are all replaceable."

So that's what Jennifer was to him. A broken toy.

It was what they all were to him. Toys. Experiments. Not people.

Penny lifted her head to smile at me encouragingly over the heads of the other, nudging her jaw in the direction of Rafe as though to tell me to *get it, girl.*

My eyes welled.

I couldn't let him kill her.

I couldn't be the reason he killed any of them. I barely knew them, but they were human. Like mom. Like so many who I'd protected from vampires for the last ten years.

This was what I trained for. Protecting humanity. Slaughtering vampires. They were my purpose. My calling was what got me from one day to the next without falling apart. Who was I if I let him hurt them to save myself?

"Do it," I muttered. "Just get it over with."

"A *wise* choice, my love."

He closed the gap between us and held out his hand. "Come sit," he beckoned, lacing the words with just enough compulsion that I was drawn to take his proffered hand and follow him numbly to the largest bed in the wide space. He sat and looked down at the spot next to him. I fell into place, my knees pressed painfully tight together. My shoulders rigid.

I lifted my wrist to him, but he clucked his tongue. "I had another vein in mind," he said, and pulse quickened. "Take off your pants."

This time, there was no compulsion in his words. He wanted me to do it willingly.

"If you *touch* me," I started, my voice an animal snarl.

He pressed a hand to his chest in mock insult. "I'm a gentleman, Rose," he said. "Besides, I have *seven* other wives to satisfy *those* desires. However, I think you'll find it will be *you* who desires *me* in just a moment. You might even beg for it. And who would I be to refuse you?"

"Never."

"We shall see," he sing-songed, his expression hardening all at once. "Now," he growled. "Take off your pants. I'm running out of patience."

When I still didn't move, he called over Luz from the carpet and my heart jumped into my throat. "No. Stop," I managed. "Okay. Fine. I'll do it."

"Wait there," he told Luz and she stopped a mere three paces away from the bed. He leaned into my side and whispered against my neck. "Just in case you get any ideas…"

I leaned back away from his face and against the silky blankets, unbuttoning my pants and peeling them from my clammy legs. When I was finished, I sat there in nothing but a thong and the tank top, feeling utterly exposed even though there were seven naked women in the room with me.

"Very good, now lean back."

I did as he said, squeezing my eyes closed.

The fact that he needed me and therefore would not drain me dry was a small comfort.

His long fingers found my thighs, opening them wide as I felt the press of him against the bed between them as he lowered himself.

My hands fisted the blankets.

This is good, I told myself. *My blood won't do anything, and he'll be distracted long enough for me to—*

Shit. Blank walls. Blank white walls. Build them higher. I cleared my mind until the raucous beating of my mortal heart in my skull was the only sound.

The warmth of his breath against my inner thigh made me cringe away, but Raphael only dug his fingers in harder, forcing my leg to still in the position he wanted.

You will not feel anything, I told myself, willing it to be true. I wouldn't allow myself to be aroused by his bite. I would not succumb to it.

I wouldn't—

His teeth sank deep into my flesh and the explosion of endorphins made my body jerk to life. My breath came in a long, strangled gasp as he began to suckle at my thigh, kneading the soft flesh there with his teeth and his lips. Squeezing hard with his fingers.

A warmth blossomed in my belly and grew until it was a hot, twirling flame. A fiery tornado of desire I fought with *everything* I had inside of me. The bedding tore where I gripped it, afraid to let go. Afraid that if I did, I would touch him. Not attack him. Touch him.

My pussy throbbed in tune with my pulse and my breasts hardened as his ancient venom did its work to undo me. I moaned, arching my back and pressing my thigh more firmly against his mouth, forcing his fangs in deeper, shivering as more venom was released into my bloodstreams.

One hand came out of the bedding and reached down of its own accord, snaking into the soft tendrils of his hair.

My vision blurred and my head swam.

Soft.

He was so soft.

I wanted…

I wanted him to touch me.

Why wasn't he touching me?

I whimpered, a plea on the verge of escaping my lips. I fisted my hand into his hair, pressing him down against me. A low growl purred against my flesh as he readjusted his fangs, lapping at my thigh with his hot tongue.

His left hand reached up, pushing incrementally up my

thigh towards my wet pussy. I bucked with feverish desire and groaned as he neared the dip at the top of my thigh, his fingers prodding at the edge of my thong.

Oh fuck.

Just as he slid one knuckle over the edge of my pussy, a moment of startling clarity washed over me. The touch of him *there* was enough to jar me back into reality just for a second.

But a second was all I needed.

With one hand fisted in his hair, I reached back and pulled the forked pin out of my hair and had the pleasure of watching his eyelids snap open a second before I drove the pin deep into the flesh of his jugular, a loud cry of violent outrage slicing through the room.

His fangs came out of my flesh and with a choking sound, he fell to the floor. I was on top of him in an instant, straddling him as my hands dove for the hair pin. He sputtered, clawing at his jugular. The instant I removed the pin, I had it sunk down into his chest.

He was stunned. Choking on his own blood. He hadn't been able to stop me.

The pin was long, but I didn't know if it was long enough to pierce his heart, so I pushed with everything I had until I had the entirely of the thing embedded in his chest cavity along with the tips of my fingers, pushing it as far as I dared.

With a great swipe of his arm, my body flew off him. It was like the hit of a metal bat and I was the ball. I pinged off the wall and landed in a tangle of limbs atop a fluffy white cushion in the corner, at least ten feet away from where he lay dying.

His eyes were wide in horror as he tore at the fabric of his thin navy shirt, exposing the wound I'd inflicted on his chest.

Raphael's wives flew into action, fluttering around him like bees around a hive. I did nothing but wait. He should have been dead already, but maybe it would just take a second.

He was the oldest vampire alive. Strongest.

Panting, I dug my fingers into the cushion, trying to see between the gyrating bodies of the monster's captives to witness the exact moment when the life left his eyes. My upper back aches painfully from where he tossed me into the wall, and I struggled for unrestricted breath as the air finally, gloriously, came back into my shriveled lungs.

But after a moment that felt an eternity, the crying of the wives began to stop, traded in for sounds of relief. Has his compulsion lifted? Were they free?

My heart soared and I eyed the door. Could we all walk out of here?

But a masculine cough crushed my hope.

No fucking way.

Raphael staggered to his feet, huffing as he dug his own fingers into the jagged slit in his chest and drew out the hair comb, letting it fall to the carpet.

No.

No this isn't possible.

I felt the comb pierce the hard muscle of his heart. *I know I did*. He should be dead. He has to be dead.

But his furious gaze fell on me and his lip curled back in a snark and I realized with a start that he was *very* much alive.

A strangled sound came out of my throat and I scrambled off the cushion, making a run for the bathroom. For my only other weapon. I'd like to see him survive a fucking metal bar through his chest.

But I barely got three feet before I fell back onto my tailbone, my face stinging form where I ran smack into a wall of muscle. Raphael towered over me, spitting in his fury as he bent to tangle his hand like a fist in my hair, if he twisted any harder, he would take some of my fucking scalp with the hair as he tore it out.

I cried out in pain and kicked out with my legs, reached out to scratch out his eyes, but it was no use. I couldn't reach him with my hands, and the blows from my feet against his sides and chest were doing absolutely nothing.

He dragged me across the floor, the carpet scraping all up my side, giving me probably the worst case of rug burn I'd ever had.

There was the metallic sound of a key in a lock and then the grip of my hair was gone, and I tasted blood in my mouth as my face collided with rough, cold cement. I blinked past the stars in my vision and spat the coppery liquid onto the ground. I was in a box. The ceiling was low, and the walls were barely my arms-length apart. I was in the solitary cell Luz had warned me about.

My heart was beating so fast I thought it might hop right out of my chest. *NO.* He couldn't leave me in here.

My chest ached painfully as the pressure of the surrounding walls threatened to suffocate me. Raphael was hunched in the doorway, his eyes promising pain.

His gaze latched onto mine and that wall I'd been carefully constructing for *hours* came smashing down in the blink of an eye. It was nothing but dust and rubble at my feet, allowing him to come crashing in, his compulsion gripping me like a vise.

"This used to be one of my brother's favorite torture methods," he spat, a hand pressing to his chest, where a small dribble of blood still leaked out of his chest. "Think of the *worst* thing you've ever had to endure."

I tried to resist but was powerless against him. An image of my mother battered and broken. Bleeding out against cold cement came unbidden to my mind.

He smiled. "Good, now I want you to *live* there. Over and over and *over* again in that memory until I decide to let you out."

My body seized as I retreated into my unconscious mind. Thrown into the memory as though I was just a kid again. As though it was happening for real, right now, all over again. I looked at my hands. My childlike hands. I looked at my mom beside me smiling at something I'd just said, and then I looked at the spot, just a few paces ahead, just beneath the streetlamp where Raphael would take her life.

I took a step. Another. I couldn't stop it. I couldn't speak.

I was a passenger in a memory that I could not change.

"And while you're doing that, I'm going to be fucking my *wives*," I heard Raphael faintly, his voice an echo in the memory. "And when I'm finished, you can choose one to die for your insolence."

I was dying inside. Crying on the outside. Unable to move or do anything except watch as Raphael swooped out of the shadows and fell upon us. I screamed.

"You better hope one of them is able to make me a child. If not, I will not longer have any use for you."

Distantly, I heard a metal door creak shut, and a key in a lock. But I wasn't in a concrete room, I was sobbing over the dead body of my mother as she choked out her final breath.

CHAPTER 18

$\mathcal{I}$ was screaming inside.

Just as I began to pass out, the deep jagged slice in my neck making it near impossible to breathe, I was thrown out of the memory. Sent hurtling through time and space only to land back at the start. Unmarred and walking next to my mother down the road without a care in the world.

It didn't matter how much I shouted and sobbed inside. The fourteen-year-old version of myself whose body I was trapped in could not hear me.

I couldn't close my eyes. I couldn't do anything but watch helplessly as Raphael killed her over *and over* again. The pain wasn't getting any less, the emotional or the physical. It was like it really was happening all over again each time. Losing her. The agony of having my throat and part of my chest flayed open. The suffocation. The sting of the cool night's breeze on an open wound.

I was starting to notice details now, as if I needed to

remember in even more startling clarity than I already did…

Like how she had been carrying a plastic bag filled with corner store junk food. All my favorites. Cheetos and those little sprinkle covered chocolate globs. Gatorade and red hots.

I'd forgotten why we were out on that road until Raphael put me back in this memory.

I'd forgotten how her dark hair shone with threads of violet in just the right light. Or how her eyes crinkled when she smiled. How had I forgotten that? Maybe if I just focused on her. On the fact that I was able to see her so clearly in this memory and how *good* that felt, it would make the horrible part more bearable.

I love you, mom, I thought within the confines of my younger self as I followed along beside her, heading toward the place where I would lose her forever. *I love you so much.*

She laughed at something I said, and I sobbed a little harder, the pain like a lead weight on my heart. It was the best sound in the whole world.

It was the last time I would ever hear it.

I held on. I held on for as long as I could, but as Raphael appeared from the shadows, I couldn't help it. I screamed. I screamed outside and in. I screamed until my throat was raw and my head throbbed. I screamed until I couldn't breathe. Until the force of my screams made my lungs hurt and my stomach heave. Somewhere, distantly, I was vomiting on a cold cement floor in a box in a room.

But here and now, my small hands shook as I clutched my other's sweater and sobbed into her chest.

When I attacked him, I tried to lend my younger self all the knowledge and ability I had gained. I tried to whisper to her that she wouldn't always be weak.

She would be strong.

She *would* kill him. She just had to wait. She had to bide her time.

When he slit her throat, all I saw through her eyes was the star-speckled sky above as she choked on her own blood and I whispered in her mind that I loved her, too. That I forgave her for not being able to save her mother.

It's not your fault.

It's not your fault.

CHAPTER 19

*C*oming out of the hell I'd been forced to live in for an indeterminate amount of time was like a cold slap. But the relief was insurmountable. Even jammed up in the concrete box, I couldn't help sobbing with tears of agonizing release. It was over. I was out.

But still my body trembled. I ached like I'd never ached before. As though every muscle in my body had been tensed as hard as brick for days and hung out to dry.

I could barely move. My arms and legs were locked against me in the fetal position, muscles screaming if I do much as flinched.

"I hope you've learned your lesson, my love. Welcome back to reality."

I whimpered and winced; my throat raw from screaming.

He reached into the box and I flinched back, a fresh scream scraping past my windpipe as I looked into his eyes. The eyes I watched stare down at my dying mother a thousand times.

"No," I managed, moving to press myself as far into the back wall as I could, whining and groaning as every muscle protested the movement.

"Come now, you can't stay in there forever," Raphael crooned, and a heavy sob expanded in my chest.

It was like some part of my fourteen-year-old self had imprinted on my adult mind. The part that was still me was furious. Angry. Wanting to rip Raphael and the entire universe to shreds. But the part of me that was still that scared teenage girl was terrified and I couldn't shake her. Not with the memories so fresh in my mind.

"Luz," Raphael called, and a woman's face appeared in the doorway, obscuring my view of the monster who put me there.

"Rose?" she said tentatively, very slowly reaching her hand out to me.

I shrank back, unable to help myself.

"Rose, I need you to come with me."

She tried an encouraging smile and her eyes crinkled at the corners, reminding me of someone. After a steadying breath, I was able to slide a little closer to her and take her hand.

She nodded. "That's it, just a little closer and I will help you."

"It hurts," I choked out.

"I know sweet thing. I know. We will make it better."

She managed to help me stand and pulled my body out of the cell, using her naked body to brace mine so I didn't fall. I couldn't believe the horrible pitiful sounds coming out of my mouth.

I blinked into the brightness of the room. I'd remembered it being dim, but after so long spent with my eyes squeezed shut, it was searing. I could make out the shape of Raphael like a shadow several feet away and studiously ignored him, telling myself over and over again like a mantra that he wasn't really there.

Luz walked me slowly toward the bathroom and a realized with a little stab of embarrassment that the malodorous stench of dried urine was, in fact, coming from me.

"It will be okay," Luz said in her soft voice, continuing to whisper little reassurances in both English and Spanish to me as she took me into the bathroom and helped me off with my clothes and into a warm bathtub filled with piping hot water, rose petals, and lavender scented bath salts. I cried out as I lowered myself into the tub, just trying to get through the next second. The next minute.

I heard a heavy door bang shut outside of the bathroom and jumped. "Is he gone?" I blurted, my voice hoarse and barely understandable.

Luz cocked her head at me.

"Raphael, did he leave?"

She frowned at me but left me for an instant to check. When she turned back, she had her lips pursed in an expression of disappointment. She sighed. "Yes."

I slumped deeper into the water and let out a shaky sigh of my own, wanting to cry again at how weak I was being right now.

I am The Black Rose, I told myself. *I am not this weak person.*

I am not a coward.

But every time I closed my eyes, I saw her lying there dead. And I saw him standing over her.

I felt what it was like to know that my mother was dead and that I was going to die, too.

"But he will return soon. He would not miss a day of ovulation."

I shuddered, remembering what horrors I'd awoken back into.

"We have to stop him," I implored Luz, clutching the edge of the massive tub as my muscles began to loosen. When she folded herself into a sitting position next to the tub, I trained my eyes on her and pressed with every ounce of my will. "You have to remember," I told her, weaving the words with compulsion. *"You have to.* I need your help."

Her eyes cleared, but only for an instant. It wasn't enough. Then her expression closed off. "I don't know what you mean."

My heart fell, pulse evening out as I pulled my gaze from hers.

There was a knock on the wall outside and Penny's pretty face appeared in the open archway, her blonde hair waving lightly around her cheekbones. "How is she?" she asked Luz in her sweet voice.

Luz didn't turn away from me while she answered. "She'll be alright, won't you cariña?"

It was no use. My compulsion would never be a match

for his. I was not my mother. I was strong in the sense that I could kill a man with my bare hands. But I wasn't strong of mind like she was.

"How long was I in that box," I said in barely a whisper.

"Two days," came Penny's reply.

I swallowed.

"Come Luz," Penny called. "Husband will be back soon. He'll be wanting to bed us all before the day is through."

Luz grinned. "You will be alright alone?"

"Yeah," I croaked. "Thank you."

"There is food and drink for you in the other room when you are ready."

"Could you bring it in here?"

There was no way I was going out there to watch that bastard rape seven women, even if they had no idea what was being done to them. Even if in their heads, it was something they wanted...

"Of course," Luz replied before getting back to her feet and following Penny from the room.

I released the ledge of the tub, ready to fully submerge myself in the water as though I could hide under the rose petals from all the horror surrounding me. But then I noticed the small smear of blood in the crease of my elbow.

I scrutinized it, rubbing at it with the dampened fingers of my left hand. Without food and water, my body wasn't able to fully heal the puncture wound there.

How much had he taken while I was in that nightmare? I didn't know whether to be grateful he hadn't bitten me or horrified that he'd been right there while I was unconscious. If he'd jabbed a needle into me while I was in that memory, what else could he have done to me?

If I'd had any scrap of food of liquid left in my body, I'd have vomited it up.

RAPHAEL HAD RETURNED AS PROMISED. AND I REMAINED IN the bathroom as planned. The doorless walls did little to block the sound of what was happening out there, but at least it was muted.

It didn't help me keep any food down, but it did help sharpen my mind. The emotions of disgust and rage acted as a wet stone against my broken mind, smoothing all the rough edges he's created back to their original state. Or at least as close to it as I could get... I had a horrible feeling that I would never heal properly after the torture he'd inflicted.

They came into the bathroom one by one to clean themselves off. Each not only reeking with the scent of him—of his seed but also stained with the evidence of his feeding.

Seeing them helped too. It helped me remember what I needed to do. That I had to get myself out of here. And get them away from him.

When I heard him leave, I relaxed a little in relief that he didn't come for me. That at least for now, he wasn't going to torture me anymore. And I let myself think of the guys.

A thing I hadn't let myself do until now.

It pained me to think of how worried they would be. I could imagine Frost reducing entire buildings to rubble in his frustration. And Blake throwing himself into recruiting more vampires. Killing each one who so much as insinuated they were with Rafe. And Ethan, simmering with quiet fury as he meticulously worked to create as much serum as he possible could with that little of my blood and marrow he still had.

But what pained me more was imagining that they weren't doing any of that. What if they were coming for me right now?

I prayed they weren't.

I knew Azrael wasn't that stupid. But my guys...they were ruled by their love for me just as I was by my love for them. They'd go on a suicide mission even if it meant only a one percent chance of succeeding.

Please, I sent the plea into the universe. *Please be smart.*

They would have to finish building the army they needed without me, otherwise coming to my rescue would be suicide. They wouldn't survive. Raphael had too many soldiers. Even with Azrael at their backs, I knew it would be futile. I hoped they knew it too.

And if they did, that meant they weren't coming. They wouldn't *be* coming until the army was of a size to match Raphael's. I had no idea how long that would take, but at the rate we were going before Amala snatched me off the streets of Phoenix, it was going to be a *while*.

Which meant I had two options. I could either wait and hope Raphael didn't kill any more of his wives, *or me* before they could find me. But that could mean Rafe being able to use me as leverage. I imagined several scenarios where he could use me to his advantage. Force them to stop fighting in order to save me. I couldn't allow that to happen.

Okay, so that's out.

Which left the only other possibility…

I couldn't wait to be saved. I needed to save myself.

There was no other option. Either I would get out, or I would die trying and then there would be no leverage for Raphael to use against his brother and my guys.

And hopefully my death would spur them to not stop until Raphael and every single motherfucking bloodsucker who followed him was dead.

$\mathcal{I}$ inspected the ceiling one last time before making my decision. It was either the door or go out through the ceiling tiles. But the ceiling was at least eighteen feet high and there was no way to know if I could even get up that high, if it would hold my weight, or if it would even lead anywhere helpful. And besides, once I got close enough to the ceiling to actually escape, I had no doubt the same agony that plagued me every time I drew near the door would make it impossible to climb anywhere.

It had to be the door then. He hadn't used a key when we first came inside, which meant that it shouldn't be locked. He'd compelled me and all the others not to leave, so why would he need to lock it?

I really fucking hoped I was right.

"You will ignore me," I told the fair-skinned French girl called Yvette. "You will not come near me or speak to me until I say so. If ever asked, you will say that I have been in bed sleeping."

"Yes," Yvette replied and blinked, walking away as though I was no longer there.

I couldn't uncompel them, but as long as my compulsion was not at odds with anything Raphael had compelled them to do, I could still compel them.

Too bad he'd compelled them within an inch of their lives so I couldn't force them to help me escape in any way or to distract or maim or poison him. But at least this way they wouldn't tell Raphael what I was up to, and they wouldn't bother me.

I needed every bit of concentration and focus I could get if this had any chance of succeeding.

To break Raphael's compulsion, my will needed to be stronger than his. Which it wasn't. I'd been able to withstand Azrael digging into my thoughts for short periods of time, but I'd never been able to fight against his compulsion. I didn't even know if I could.

Azrael said in time I would be able to, but time wasn't on my side here.

Once Rafe figured out that my blood—without the processing Ethan had figured out—would *not* get him what he wanted, he would have no more use for me. Maybe no more use for the women he was keeping hostage here, either. I figured I had a few weeks to before he started attempting other means of getting what he wanted.

I'd heard Grace talking to Penny earlier...

He was starting to wonder if maybe the problem was

that he couldn't impregnate a *mortal*. That maybe he needed to plant his seed in a pure blood Vocari for it to take.

We were a different species after all.

So, I had a few weeks if I was lucky. If none of the girls peed on sticks and got two lines…

Well, I didn't want to fucking imagine it.

I just needed to make sure it didn't happen.

Bottle of water in tow, I stepped slowly toward the exit door, pausing when it began to hurt. That is where I folded myself down onto the floor and crossed my legs, setting the bottle of water down beside me.

I'd eaten as much as I could last night, or whatever time of the fucking day it was. And then, despite my efforts to stay awake, I'd passed out and slept for gods knows how long, a deep, black, gloriously dreamless sleep. But if Penny was right it had been a little less than a full twenty-four hours. And when I awoke, there was a new blood smear in the crease of my arm, though this time there was no puncture wound.

My body had regained its physical strength.

Now it was time to see if my mind could withstand what I was about to put it through after everything it'd already had to endure.

I was still experiencing flashbacks every time I closed my eyes. My memories of that night painted in vivid imaged against the back of my eyelids. It was hard to keep yourself distracted in a room with zombie-women and nothing to do but bide your time.

But *this*. I was really hoping *this* would take my mind off it.

And maybe…just maybe…it would also see me free.

I breathed through the agony ripping every one of my nerve endings to shred. In through my nose and out through my mouth. I quieted my thoughts, focusing only on my will. My desire to beat him. My need to escape. I worked to make those needs and desires—the manifestations of my will *stronger* than his.

When the pain became tolerable, I took a deep breath and moved several inches closer to the door.

The pain intensified and I groaned, concentrating on my breaths and nothing else for a moment so I could stay calm. In and out.

In and out.

The pain radiated through me like a million awful sensations at once. It was burning. It was sharp. It was aching. Throbbing. It was every sort of pain you could imagine thrown at you all at once, wrapped up with a pretty bow and kick in the teeth.

"Fuck," I ground out through clenched teeth, reaching with a shaking hand to my bottle of water to take a little sip. The cool water coated my mouth and that tiny bit of bliss was enough for me to regain my concentration.

I began to meditate again. Breathing and growing the force of my will.

Then I moved another few inches and started the process again.

Sometime during the slow creep toward the door, my nose began to bleed. A steady drip of crimson fell onto my shirt. And after a while longer, I felt a wetness in my ears and felt the drip of it as it bled onto my shoulders and rolled down my neck.

My body was tearing itself apart from the inside out trying to fight his compulsion, but I didn't care.

I'd made the decision.

It was either get free or die.

And I was not going to quit. Not after waking up a shriveled husk of myself after what he put me through in that box. I hadn't even recognized myself when I'd looked in the mirror after getting out of the bath. I saw a scared little girl in my reflection. A sad version of myself I'd already defeated once before. I wouldn't allow him to reduce me back to that state.

Not a fucking chance.

I can leave, I told myself as though compelling my own mind. *I can walk out that door. I* can.

I can.

But the blood was gushing faster now than it was before from my ears and nose. And what I'd mistakenly thought were tears in my eyes turned out to be more blood, and as I blinked the red liquid spread over my eyes, tingeing everything the violent color.

My heart was thumping wildly in my chest and I knew —*I just knew*—if I didn't move, it was going to burst. Choking on the metallic tang in the back of my throat, I raised a shaky hand to my chest ad dipped my fingernail into the blood and then dragged it in a thin line over the plush carpet at my feet. As soon as I was done my lungs seized and in a last ditch effort as black spots crowded in at the corners of my vision, I scrambled backward until the pain was gone and I slumped into a puddle of exhaustion on the carpet, my eyes fluttering closed.

SEVEN FUCKING FEET.

That was all I'd managed in three days of trying. But it was something. And I was getting better at it. I could see the progress from the small markings I'd left in blood each step of the way. The first was about three feet closer than I'd ever gotten before starting this little experiment. The second mark was nearer to four feet. And the newest mark. The one I'd left before dragging my aching body back to where it didn't hurt was at about *seven* feet.

From that mark to the door there was only about three more feet of space. I could do it. I knew I could. Even though getting to the point of seven feet was like hitting a solid wall of excruciating agony. I'd actually screamed a little at how intense it was.

But I *could* do it.

My only worry was that when I finally made it to the door—when I opened it and stepped outside—that the pain would continue.

He told me I couldn't leave this room. So, once I'd left it—once I'd *beaten* him—his compulsion should *theoretically* fade.

But I really had no fucking idea what would happen. I'd never broken Azrael's compulsion before, so I had nothing to go on but blind hope in my crazy plan.

I was leaving tomorrow.

I had to eat and sleep and wash the blood off my face and neck before Rafe came back.

He hadn't been here in a few days, but there was no telling how much longer he would stay away. And the girls had taught me how to keep track of time.

There was a furnace on a timer. It kicked on in the evening around the time food was dropped off for us. And it kicked off again a few hours later, closer to the time a lot of the girls went to sleep. There was only one meal delivery per day so I couldn't use any other meals to help me tell the time.

The only other thing that denounced the hour was the chiming of a bell. It was so faint you could barely hear it, but when I asked Grace what the sound was yesterday, she told me it was the only city hall clock tower and that it chimed on the hour and on the half hour.

The old city hall clock tower in New York City.

Which meant me were right in the thick of it. If I could just get outside in daylight, I would have a solid thirteen or fourteen hour head start before he would be able to come after me.

There was the problem of Amala to contend with, but I'd just have to find a way to deal with that. Surely if I just kept moving, she wouldn't be able to track me to one location and go there.

The only reason she found me in Phoenix was because Azrael told her exactly where we were going in case we needed her help. What a joke. I really fucking hoped he didn't tell her where he was keeping the vampires we'd managed to rally to our side. That he didn't ask her to ward that building at any point their *friendship*.

If she was on Raphael's side and she knew where we were keeping them, it would be bye-bye army and we'd have to start from scratch.

I shook my head and Luz tugged on my hair, trying to keep my head steady as she continued putting the tight French braid into my black hair.

"If you had not stabbed husband with the comb, we would still have them," she griped. "Now hold still."

"*Ow.*"

He'd made Luz go into the bathroom and collect them all after he'd stuffed me in the box. Now we had only Luz's deft fingers and skill at crafting braids with what she called *natural ties* to keep them fixed in place. Basically, she let the hair tangle at the ends instead of pulling it apart after each weave and then turned the knotted section of hair into itself at the end of the braid, forming a sort of extra strong knot that help the braid in place.

Thank fuck because as much as I loved my hair, having it in my face twenty-four seven would have had be shearing it off the first chance I got.

"There," she said and moved her hands from my hair to my shoulders, spinning me to look at her.

I smirked.

"Beautiful," she said, and my smirk softened.

Her warm brown eyes roved over my face and then she called for Poppy to come over and have her wild red hair braided next.

I stood and watched the two of them sitting on the floor. Luz on a fluffy cushion near a sconce on the wall, and Poppy cross legged in front of her, smiling.

There was one flaw with my plan.

It didn't include any way to take them with me.

I'd been trying to come up with something every waking moment other than the time I'd spent inching toward the door or sleeping—or, more accurately, passed out from exhaustion.

I compelled Luz and Grace and Penny and all the others. I'd *been* compelling them every day. Praying that if I compelled them as forcefully as I could each and every day to forget every order Raphael had ever given them that maybe, just maybe, my compulsion would win out.

If I just kept at it.

But I could see it wasn't any use, no matter how much I deluded myself into thinking it would work. None of them seemed even mildly affected by my efforts to release the hold Rafe had on each of their minds.

And so long as they were compelled by him, they wouldn't come with me.

Which meant that Azrael's plan to take down Rafe *had* to work. And fast. Because I would be back for them. One way or another, I wouldn't leave them here to rot.

I'd have Azrael remove Rafe's compulsion and make them forget the horrible things they'd endured. They'd go home. Wherever home was for each of them. And they'd go back to their lives.

And if they didn't have lives waiting for them, I'd make

Azrael see to it that they were able to start fresh ones. Happy ones.

Ones where the taint of Raphael would never touch them again.

"I saved you some of the cake," Penny said, coming up behind me.

I usually waited until they were all finished with their meals before I ate whatever was left.

I turned to her with a tight throat and stared down at the slab of chocolate cake in her outstretched hands. Her bright blue eyes watched me curiously. "Are you upset?" she asked.

I shook my head, trying to jar myself out of my head as I took the cake. "No," I told her, forcing a small grin. "Thank you, Penny."

She perked up and spun, her blonde hair twirling around her heart-shaped face as she skipped back to where the others were all sat around a large platter of food.

A crippling pang of guilt almost brought me to my knees. When the time came, would I be able to leave them?

My chest ached.

You're no good to them dead, I reminded myself.

And soon, when Rafe realized my blood wasn't working, that was exactly what I would be.

The faint sound of footsteps in the hallway alerted me that he was coming. But today, there was a second set of footsteps with him.

I rushed to sit with the group, hoping to conceal my

mind among theirs as I constructed my mental barriers, closing my eyes to focus. Working fast, I got it good and solid by the time the door clicked open and they stepped inside the room, but still I was adding bricks and supports, pushing it higher and thicker. Stronger.

He'd blown through my other barriers with the smallest shove last time. I intended not to make it so easy for him this time.

Sweat beaded on my brow and my jaw twitched.

Beside Raphael in the doorway was Amala.

Fucking traitorous bitch.

I was immediately seething with rage at the mere sight of her and couldn't believe that only a couple weeks ago she was *healing* me and warding Azrael's house.

The house that Raphael now knew the location of, I realized with a start, chiding myself for not realizing that bit of information before.

Fuck.

I hoped they didn't go back there. Or that they'd had time to evacuate everyone.

Oh my god...*Ethan*...

It was like a knife twisting in my chest. *He got out*, I told myself. *He's completely fine. You'll see him soon.* I prayed it was the truth because I couldn't live with the alternative.

I calmed myself with the knowledge that Raphael would have been sure to rub it in if he'd killed Ethan. He would have used the information to break me, I had no doubt.

But Estelle was in there, too. My throat constricted at the thought of the spindly old woman harmed in any way.

And Valentina.

And the vampires we'd converted.

Damn.

Nothing you can do until you're free.

Don't think about it.

Don't dwell.

Focus, Rose.

Focus.

I peered up at the pair of them nearing us from across the room from under my lashes and flinched when I caught sight of his face. My body shuddered as flashes of the memories bombarded my mind. My breaths hitched and my hands began to shake.

I tried hard to stop them, to calm my body before it could go into full panic attack, but it was so much harder than I thought it would be.

One look at him and I was back *there*. Back on the sidewalk under the streetlamp, lying next to my dead mother as I choked on my own blood.

I curled my hands into fists, pressing my nails hard against the inside of my palms, using the sting to shake me out of it.

After another second, I managed to get a hold on myself. I was still trembling and could do nothing to stop it, but the panic attack I'd felt surfacing from the well of darkness at my core had re-submerged into the pit.

I will not be this person, I reminded myself.

I wouldn't become the scared girl I was ten years ago. I'd already defeated her. I wasn't going to do it twice.

Steeling myself, I forced my head up and I looked at him head on, swallowing past the lump in my throat.

The girls rose one by one to greet him with embraces and small kisses. I remained where I was, my eyes boring a hole into his head. Once they were finished and returned to sitting around the meal tray, Rafe turned his sights on me.

"What?" he asked in a velvety soft voice dripping with sarcasm. "No welcome from my favorite Rose?"

I clenched my jaw.

"And I thought we were beginning to get along..."

I resisted the urge to launch myself at his face and scratch his eyes out, but just barely. If I'd learned anything being here and being with Azrael, it was that I was no match for them. And would never be—physically at least. Mentally? Well, I was starting to have hope that one day I might be.

Just a few more feet to the door.

Raphael narrowed his eyes at me, and I remembered to clear my mind. I thought only of what was happening right here and now and nothing else.

"What is *she* doing here?" I all but hissed, a foul taste coating my tongue.

Raphael gestured to Amala and I took in her form. The soft curves beneath her long, heavy-looking jade green dress. Her flawless wet-sand skin and mane of near-black hair. Once, I'd thought her beautiful. Now I only saw the predator in her bleached brown eyes. I only saw the feral nature of her soul.

As though on que, Amala, ignoring my inquiry, moved to kneel at the other end of the naked women around the platter and turned herself to Penny. The witch reached out her hands and placed them on her belly.

I jolted, my body about to launch into defense of the blonde girl I was starting to think of as something of a little sister.

It was Luz's hand that steadied me as she folded herself into a seated position next to me on the carpet. My nostrils flared.

"What is she—"

"No," Amala said ominously and Penny, confused, bowed her head. "This one is not pregnant."

Dawning realization slapped me. He was having Amala check to see if any of them had been impregnated.

But...wouldn't Amala know about the serum Ethan was making? I didn't often see Amala around the house. In fact, other than when she'd healed me, I hadn't seen her at all. But surely, she knew?

Unless...unless Azrael had been lying about how much he trusted her. Had he compelled her to stay away? Or to forget what Ethan was doing?

My head was starting to hurt. This wasn't right. How did these people keep up with all the possibilities born of magic in their heads?

Was *anything* possible?

Amala moved to Grace next, placing her hands against the ebony skin of her long stomach.

"No," she said again, and moved to the next.

I thought I would have more time.

It took weeks for a pregnancy test to work, didn't it?

I hadn't accounted for Amala being able to tell whether there was a pregnancy within days.

Which meant that I didn't have as much time as I thought I did.

I didn't have any time left at all.

A sick feeling coiled in my gut and a cold finger ran down my spine.

With each of the girls Amala checked for pregnancy and denied there being one, Rafe's expression hardened. More and more until it was twisted, his curled upper lip twitching. His shoulders rising with tension.

This was not good.

Finally, Amala was directly next to me and placing her hands against Luz's belly. It took everything I had not to reach out and strangle her. She was so close. It was possible I could snap her neck before Rafe would be able to stop me.

Amala had her eyes closed, concentrating as she used her magic to feel for the spark of life in Luz's belly. A spark she wouldn't find. Surely, she knew what that would mean...

Amala would know what Raphael was planning to do if my blood didn't allow him to bear a child with a mortal. A cold sweat broke out over my chest as Amala's dull brown eyes snapped open, finding mine for an instant before they darted away.

She removed her hands from Luz's belly and turned to

Raphael. "This one," she said. "The life is weak. Fragile. But it is there."

Raphael pressed his hand over his face as though overwhelmed with an emotion I knew he wasn't capable of possessing.

While his face was covered and the room broke out into animated whispers, my attention turned back to Amala, who was staring at me with a look I couldn't read.

A hard, piercing look that I knew was meant to convey something, but I wasn't understanding. She looked to Luz for a heartbeat and back to me. She shook her head once, the motion so small it was almost imperceptible. Then she rose and it was like whatever I'd imagined happened between us just then was a figment of my imagination.

I cleared my head. Both wanting to believe and not wanting to believe what I thought she was trying to tell me. But I couldn't let myself think about it. Not now. Not with Rafe only a few feet away.

Raphael swooped in close, drawing Luz off the floor and into his one-armed embrace, crushing her head against the crook of his shoulder. When he released her, he looked straight into her eyes and said, "Come," in a tone I knew was one he used to compel. "You will remain with me now."

Luz beamed at him and my heart sank.

"The pregnancy is still young. It may not remain viable," Amala's voice came from across the room where she stood sentinel by the door.

Rafe turned on her with a wicked sneer. His breathing

heavier for a moment before he regained a measure of calm.

"I would advise you to keep the others," she continued, her hand moving to the door handle. "In case this pregnancy fails."

Amala opened the door and stepped out into the hall, holding it open for Raphael to accompany her. "You will do everything you can to see it through," he growled at her as he passed.

"Luz," Penny called, her chin quivering and her eyes dangerously close to tears.

Luz turned back to us for an instant before the door shut behind them, her face the picture of radiance. Of complete and utter bliss. She smiled back at Penny, and at us all.

I choked on a sob as she and Rafe and Amala vanished from view because I understood now what Amala had done.

Luz wasn't pregnant at all.

I didn't know why she was helping me, but Amala had just sacrificed Luz to give me a chance to escape. To give me more time before Raphael tried to plant his seed within *me*. For me to have a chance to save the others.

When Raphael learned Luz had *'lost'* the pregnancy, he'd kill her. I had no doubt.

And I'd *let* her go.

I looked at all the other girls. They were hopeful for Luz, and a bit sad to have lost a sister wife. Luz had been like a mother to them all. I scooted closer to Penny and took her ivory hand in mine.

She looked at me, blinking back tears. "She's gone," the young girl said in a watery voice.

I nodded, trying to contain my own riotous emotions as I readied myself for what I had to do next. If Luz was going to die, there was no way in *hell* I would let it be in vain. And when I got them all out of here, they would know that it was Luz who saved them. Not me.

CHAPTER 21

I compelled them all again. I hated doing it, but it was the only way.

The six remaining women in Raphael's den of captives would now tell Raphael that I was *occupied* in the bathroom if he asked for my whereabouts. They would not offer this information unless asked, and they would not permit him to enter the bathroom unless he pushed them.

The only way he would know I was gone was if he forced his way into the bathroom or forced one of them to *fetch* me. Or if he figured out that I compelled them I suppose he could just undo my compulsion with his own stronger version.

Sighing, I readied myself to leave. I wasn't going to turn back this time. I was making to that door, and I was going to go through it, no matter how much it hurt. No matter how much it felt as though my heart would burst in my chest. Death or freedom.

I would have one or the other today.

ELENA LAWSON

No more time to waste.

My plan only had to work long enough for me to get to Azrael. And occupied as he was with Luz, I imagined he wouldn't be bothering with us until he found the pregnancy to be a sham. Which, I figured, meant I had at least a few days.

If he brought in an actual doctor at that point or forced her to use a pregnancy test, then he would be back to try again.

I had no idea where my guys were. Where Azrael was. I had to assume they weren't at his home in Italy since Amala knew where that was, but for all I knew they could be some place in Europe anyway.

Though I doubted they would've left the United States without me. In fact, I was banking on it. Without any belongings or a passport, it would be a challenge to compel my way onto an aircraft bound for the EU. Not impossible. But a headache I didn't want to have to endure if I survived this part of the journey.

I needed to get out, in daylight, and find a phone.

But that wouldn't really help me, either, would it?

I didn't know any of the guys' numbers by heart.

Get out, I told myself. *Step one.*

Figure out the rest once you're free.

There was a snide voice in the back of my mind telling me that if I didn't have a solid plan once I got out of here then I was royally fucked...but I decided to tell that little voice to shut the fuck up so I could focus.

"I'm coming back," I told them, even though I'd made it so they wouldn't remember this, or me leaving at all. "I am going to come back and take you all away from here."

They regarded me with mixed expressions of curiosity, upset, and confusion.

"But we don't want to leave," insisted Frances. She didn't talk often, and I'd almost forgotten that she was French.

It seemed Raphael had chosen his women not only for their beauty, but for *variety*.

"I know," I told Frances, my stomach clenching. There really wasn't anything I could say that would help. I only told them I was coming back aloud to make myself believe it. They wouldn't even remember.

I was telling myself what I needed to hear so I could leave them here to continue to be defiled and compelled. It was breaking something inside me—the mere thought of leaving them.

Abandoning them, my mind whispered. *You're abandoning them.*

I shook my head hard and swallowed. I wasn't abandoning them. Leaving was the only way to save them.

I brushed my hand over Penny's hair and smiled at her to try to draw a return smile from her frowning lips. She gave me a half-hearted grin I was going to have to accept.

Once I said goodbye that would be it. They would all believe I was in the bathroom. They wouldn't see me or hear me. They wouldn't wonder where I was. They would just know that I was in the bathroom if asked and that's it.

I met each of their eyes, drawing from their hazed expressions the strength—*the indignant fury*—I would need to power my resolve. "Goodbye," I said in a hard tone.

As one they blinked. And when my compulsion settled into their minds, they began to wander away as if I was never there. Grace to the vanity in the corner to rub some cream into her skin. Penny to the spot where Luz usually braided the girls' hair, where she found the brush laying on the carpet and began to brush her own hair even though it already looked smooth as ever.

The others went to pick at the remnants of last night's supper around the silver tray before they would wander to bed. I'd been keeping track of the chiming of the city hall bell since the food was dropped off and the furnace had kicked on in the evening. If I hadn't missed any bells, and I didn't think I had, then it had been six hours.

I didn't know what time of the evening the furnace kicked on exactly, but just knowing it was evening helped. Raphael, if he came to us, it was usually after dark, and that was generally a few hours after the food came.

So, my assumption was that the daily meal arrived around six in the evening. And Raphael usually arrived around nine. Since it had been six hours since the meal came for us, dropped off by a burly bald vampire with a scar through his face, I had to imagine it was close to midnight.

The last time I made a try for the door, I'd gotten seven feet, and it took me four hours give or take.

I had three extra feet to go today if I was going to make it out.

If my assumptions were correct, then I would be out

of that door by six in the morning. The sun should be up by then. All I needed to do was find an exit or a window that wasn't made of reinforced glass. Easy peasy, right?

I started the process by taking deep inhales of breath. I fetched the shower rod I'd dismantled almost a week ago from where I'd been keeping it beneath a long cushion closer to the door that none of the girls dared to use.

For them, getting even as close as this, where I was standing right now, was uncomfortable. For me, after all the work I'd done over the past few days fighting through Raphael's compulsion, I wasn't even flinching yet.

That made me hopeful. And maybe a little cocky.

I fucking got this shit.

Bottle of water in one hand to keep my hydrated, reducing the risk of passing out on the carpet. Makeshift bo staff in the other just in case I needed something to defend myself if this worked.

All set.

Let's do this.

THE PAIN WAS ALMOST INDESCRIBABLE. BUT I TRIED TO describe it in my mind if only to distract myself from it. At a mere foot away from the door, it was like trying to climb a mountain. But the mountain is made of jagged glass and you're naked. And the mountain is underwater, so you're suffocating. And even though you're naked and underwater, you're scorching hot, burning from the inside out as though the water is laced with rivers of scalding lava.

The blood clogging my throat and spilling down my neck from ears and my cheeks from my eyes told me I may not make it. My head was throbbing in time with the insane beating of my heart. I could barely breath.

I was painfully aware of the pitiful sounds I was making, but I stopped giving a shit about that five feet ago.

One. More. Foot.

My will is stronger.

I can beat him.

My will is stronger.

I can *beat him.*

My stomach roiled and a wave of vertigo washed over me, making my body teeter to one side, but I bit back the bile in my throat. I couldn't leave a massive pile of vomit a foot away from the door. He would know I'd left as soon as he opened it. Or when his lackey's brough in the food platter tomorrow, they would see it and tell him.

I could leave no trace of my exit. But I was bleeding so much from my ears and nose that I thought there had to have been at least a few drops in the carpet by now. I had to hope they didn't seem suspicious. Rafe liked to feed on his *wives* when he fucked them. There were minute blood stains all over the carpet, and the deep burgundy color hid them well.

They would hide mine, too.

My mouth was dry and tasted of bile. I'd have killed someone for just one more sip of the water I'd finished two feet ago—literally *killed* a person.

"*Fuck,*" I ground out as I moved my body another few

inches, doing my best to wet my lips with whatever moisture I had left.

If I could just stand up...

I could reach the door handle from here.

I wanted to sag with relief. Or cry. Or...something.

But I couldn't do any of those things. If I broke
concentration, even for a second, the pain would wipe me
out. I could already sense the cloying embrace of oblivion
pandering at the edges of my conscious mind, beckoning
me to let go. To give in and fall unconscious from the
exertion and the pain.

I couldn't let it happen until this was finished.

The floor wavered beneath me as I set the bo staff
down beside me and pushed my body forward and dug
my fingernails into the carpet, pushing my body up. Stab-
bing bolts of agony shot up my arms and I staggered.

I needed the handle to help me up. Using one arm to
support me, I reached up with the other, quietly
screaming through the thunderous roar of blood in my
ears. I could barely make out the shape of it through the
sheen of red coating my eyes.

My hand closed around the cool metal and all once the
world came into focus. It was like a rubber band had been
pulling and pulling *and pulling* all around me as I dragged
myself to the door, and the instant I hit my goal, it
snapped into place. Air rushed into my lungs and stars
danced along the edges of my periphery. I cried out at the
absence of pain, tears replacing the blood in my tear
ducts.

My body shook against the icy metal of the door. I

didn't dare let go of the handle, afraid if I did the pain would all rush back in to finish me off. If it did, I didn't think I would survive it.

I couldn't be sure how long I sat there, slumped against the door. Longer than I should've, that much was sure. But once I finally found the strength to get to my feet, the shaking had settled to a slight tremble. My breaths were even and slow. And my hand was utterly numb around the door handle.

I inched the metal rod from the shower closer with my foot and lifted it into my grasp, finding my fingers clumsy and feeling oddly detached.

Now was the moment of truth.

If this door was locked, I was basically fucked.

I closed my eyes for a minute, letting myself revel in the fact that I actually *fucking beat Raphael*, and then I glanced one more time back at the woman I was leaving behind. They were all asleep, as though there hadn't been another person bleeding and grunting and cursing just across the room.

I drew in a sharp breath and spun, pulling the door open in one quick motion. There was resistance, the door was fucking heavy as hell, but it opened and beyond it the white hallway stretched on to freedom.

CHAPTER 22

*T*he silence outside of the room was suffocating. I was afraid to breathe to loudly in case someone would hear. It took me nearly a full minute just to close the door so it wouldn't make a sound. Once it was fully shut, I moved into the corridor. My bare feet made little noise as I crept along toward a bend in the hall.

Once I got to it, there were two options, one, go back the way I remembered coming from with Rafe...but I knew that only lead to his penthouse chambers and locked patio doors with reinforced glass.

I wouldn't make that same mistake twice.

So left it was. I swallowed my trepidation and kept my breaths shallow, clutching the metal rod to my chest. I could still hardly believe I'd defeated his compulsion. Now was the part I was worried about. The part I should have planned better.

But how could I when I had no idea where the exits

were? I got out of the room. Now I still needed to get out of the building. And into the solace of the sun.

Fuck. fuck. Fuck.

I'd been around three corners and all I'd found was more white walled hallway. More fluorescent lights that stung my eyes. There were doors here and there, but I didn't dare open any. What if this was where Raphael's soldiers were housed? What if behind all of those doors were nests of sleeping vampires?

I shuddered. I fucking hoped not. The blood on my face and neck was still a bit tacky. If any woke, they'd smell it and come looking for a snack.

My fingers ached where they curled around the metal. My palms damp from clammy sweat.

Damnit, where was the fucking—

Exit sign!

A big ass illuminated sign was placed on the ceiling outside of a door at the other end of the hallway I'd just entered. My eyes were still adjusting to the bright, but it clearly said *exit* it big, bright red letters.

My heart soared and I loosened my vise-like grip on the pole. My body was still weak and clumsy from what I'd put it through back in the room, but the spark of relief at finding the exit was helping to sharpen my focus.

A noise somewhere in the building from where I'd just come made me stop breathing entirely. It was distinct. The creaking sound of a door opening. The solemn click of it shutting again.

I looked back toward where the sound was emanating from, flinching when I heard heavy-soled footsteps. I couldn't tell yet if they were coming this way or not. I turned back to the exit. Did I run?

If I ran, I'd make it there before any vamp who came after hearing the drum of my running steps, but then what? Could I make it all the way down to the ground level faster than whoever it was?

I knew I probably couldn't. Not in the state I was in now. Which meant I really only had two options; hope the vamp didn't come this way and kill it if it did. *Quietly*.

But all it would take is one shout from the vamp before I attacked, and he'd have the whole building descending upon us. He'd have *Rafe* descending upon me.

That couldn't happen. I didn't come this far to—

The footsteps were *definitely* coming this way now. There was a sharp knock. Then another door opening, this one closer.

The distant sound of garbled whispers.

I was inching closer to the exit door now, eager to get into the stairwell before they came around the bend and it was too late.

I ran on tip toes toward it and when I reached out to the handle, the metal pole jostled forward and knocked against the frame of the door like a gong.

A gasp flew from my lips before I could contain it, followed by a string of muttered curses as I wrenched the door open. There was no sense in trying to stay quiet anymore.

I caught sight of them just as I passed over the threshold, two burly fuckers, one I recognized to be the vamp who was currently on meal delivery duty in the wives' chambers. I pulled the door shut, my heart in my throat, and in a reflexive response, decided to shove the metal shower pole through the handle on the other side. It jammed against a wall and I knew with enough jostling it would come free. I braced one side against the door, getting leverage from where the bar was pushed through the handle and reefed on the other side, muscles straining.

I managed to bend the metal rod half a foot from the rush of adrenaline coursing through my muscles. At the new angle, they wouldn't be able to get though unless they tore it down. Just as I released the bar, the door banged against it and the grunt of a vamp on the other side told me they knew I was there. It was only a matter of time before Rafe knew, too.

Fuck.

So much for my head start.

"Go down to the next floor," A gruff voice barked on the other side, spurring me back into motion. I spun, finding the stairwell split into two directions. Up and down. A sign on the wall to my left, leading up, said *Roof Access.*

I looked down, wondering how long I had before the other vamp—before a fucking horde of them—would have this stairwell filled. I couldn't go down.

"Godfuckingdamnit," I cursed and took the stairs two at a time all the way up. I could already hear the echo of vampires below, their rapid footfalls sounding like rain on a tin roof in the echoing space.

I rushed the last few steps and burst free of the door, taking a massive lungful of warm smoggy New York air. I tripped outside, falling to scrape my knees on the rough rooftop and scrambling back to my feet and away from the exit door.

Frantically, I hurried to the ledge, throwing myself against it for support. I peered over into the barely there light of early morning. I searched the sky for sun and found none. It was there, just below the horizon, but it wasn't casting its glow over the building yet. I couldn't tell how much more time it would take—there were too many buildings blocking my view of the skyline.

No.

A crashing sound echoed up from the empty doorway I'd just exited, and I scanned the street below the building —searching for a way out. A fire escape. A swimming pool I could jump into. *Fucking anything.*

But it seemed that kind of luck was only for people in the movies. Hot, frustrated tears stung my eyes and when the first vampire stepped hesitantly out onto the roof, I did the only thing I could think of—I jumped up onto the ledge.

"Come a fucking inch closer and I'll jump," I spat, feral.

The big fucker froze, and he threw his arm out like a bar to stop the others from exiting onto the roof, too.

"Where's Rafe?" he asked the others in a harsh whisper, not allowing them to pass.

"He's coming," came a reply from somewhere among the horde of angry vampires.

That meant I didn't have long. I peeled my gaze away from them for an instant, looking behind me one more time, praying there would be something—some way for me to survive the fall. It had to be close to fifteen stories. I'd survived a drop from ten once. I'd even landed on my feet—though I broke them both along with my femurs.

Could I survive it? Would they have time to come and collect my broken body from the pavement before the sun rose?

A shimmer of sunlight on glass caught my eye to the right, and a sliver of hope lodged itself in my chest. If I just waited them out, then maybe…

"He's in the stairwell," the words were like a round fired from a gun, sending me shooting down the narrow ledge—toward the little glimmer of sunlight. To freedom or to death.

He would *not* take me. Not again.

My arms pumped at my sides and the blaring of car horns and whir of engines in the street below were the only sounds I could hear. There was shouting, too. Lots of it. But I was ignoring that.

My breaths were strong and steady, my pulse a thunderous roar. The next building was over fifteen feet away, it's only a couple of feet lower than the one I was on. *Too far*, my mind whispered.

"I can make it," I hissed between pants. The sun stained the panes of glass on the edge of the eastern face of it in blinding gold. But still the rooftop where I stood was in shadow.

A bellow unlike anything I'd ever heard roared in dissonant fury behind me. It was the shove I needed to throw myself from the building's ledge. I screamed as my body left the ground and soared through the air. I reached, willing my body to breech the gap.

But I was falling too fast. The moment I realized I wasn't going to make it, I looked down, screeching like a mother fucking banshee as the traffic-choked asphalt stared back up at me in startling clarity.

I readied my body for impact, bracing, ready to tuck and roll the instant the balls of my feet connected with the roof of the taxi-cab it looked like I was going to land on top of if traffic didn't move.

"*Fuuuuuuuuuckkkkkk*," the curse was long and swallowed up by the crisp wind whipping all around me. I closed my eyes just before impact, pulling my arms into my chest to roll, praying I'd get away with minimal breakage when something hit me from the side, snatching me up out of mid-air and sending me sprawling to the ground amid traffic.

My body rolled along the gritty asphalt and I came up bloodied and sputtering, but not broken. Not dead.

I opened my eyes and stared up at the sun streaked sky, laughing as a ribbon of warm golden light caressed my cheek. I didn't give a flying fuck that every car around my body laying spread-eagle on the ground was honking. That the drivers of the nearest vehicles were shouting, their shapes drawing near to get a better look at me.

I laughed until my throat was choked with heavy sobs and I couldn't laugh anymore.

You fucking crazy bitch, I told myself. *You total fucking psycho.*

"Rose?" The voice was broken and breathless, but I

recognized it in an instant. His face appeared over mine, blocking out the sunlight while New York shouted and honked all around us.

Ethan's hair shone like it was spun from pure sunlight. His steeped tea eyes regarded me with a mixture of relief and horror as he bent over me, his hands fluttering over me as though he were terrified to touch me. As though he didn't think I was real.

"Oh fuck," I managed around a thick throat and the taste of blood on my tongue from where I'd bitten it good and fucking hard. "I'm dead, aren't I? I didn't survive the fall."

I dropped my head and sniffed. "Well that's fucking shitty. Are you dead t—"

"Rose," Ethan urged, kneeling to lift the back of my skull from the pavement with the gentle press of his fingers on the back of my head. "Are you hurt? Can you move?"

There was so much worry in his voice. Too much. Why worry if we were dead? Could I even *be* hurt anymore now?

The garbled sound of sirens several blocks away and the blaring of a fire-engine's horn assaulted my ears. Why were there sirens in hell?

Then Ethan winced, a sharp barking sound churning from his lips as the sunlight came through the cracks in the building and painted him fully in its light. The exposed skin on his cheek and neck began to redden.

"What the fuck?" I heard myself say and flinched from

the angry road rash all along the side of my arm as I pushed myself up onto my scraped elbows.

"Eth?"

"You aren't dead Rose," he managed through grunts as he dipped his head low into the shadow of the blue SUV honking and trying to inch forward in front of us. Fucking dickheads. Couldn't they see there were people in the road?

Reality came crashing down on me like a ton of bricks. I was up and thumping on the hood of the vehicle in the blink of an eye, shouting profanity at the driver.

Ethan's hand closed around mine and I flew into action, leaving the asshole driver to pull him in a weaving pattern through cars and trucks, around trash bins and eventually, through the doors of a shopping plaza.

He groaned and gritted his teeth the whole way, muttering something about how it's been three days since he last dosed himself with the serum and he was lucky he didn't burn to a crisp trying to save me from that fall.

What a fucking *fool*.

He could have died.

Once we were safely inside, I pulled him away from curious onlookers and into an unoccupied family restroom, letting go only once the door was closed behind us.

"What the hell were you thinking?" I shouted at him, breathless and teary-eyed and brimming with too many emotions to express all at once.

He's really here.

This is real.

I'm not dead.

Ethan lifted a brow at me, and the redness on his flesh began to dull back to pink and then fade back to normal, his vampire body healing itself in seconds, leaving his smooth pale skin perfect as ever. Completely unblemished.

"I was expecting a much different response," he replied, his handsome pace pinching in confusion. "We've been watching that fucking building from a safe distance since you were captured, *praying* you would somehow find a way out—*trying* to find a safe way *in*. We—"

The space between us vanished as I launched myself at him, pulling him hard against me, burying my face in his warm, solid chest. The tears flowed freely then, soaking my cheeks and his shirt with their hot wetness. His arms came around me and his face pressed into my hair. He stroked my back and pressed his fingers through the hair at the back of my neck to hold me there against him.

"It's okay," he said, unable to conceal the shock in his voice. I didn't think he'd ever seen me like this. Not ever. It made me want to try to get a hold on myself, but I only ended up crying harder.

"Rose," he nudged in a whisper, the word a hard choke. He paused, and I got the sense he was afraid to ask. I wished he wouldn't. "What happened in there?"

When I didn't answer him, instead continuing to sob until the tears became fewer and my breaths evened out. He just held me. He didn't ask any more questions. He was just *there*. And it was exactly what I needed.

"We should go," he whispered at my ear, brushing the

hair away from my face as I leaned back to get another good look at him. "The guys were with Azrael, cutting it close to sunrise this time, but they'll be back at the apartment by now and wondering where I went."

I sighed in relief. They were all alright then. That was all that mattered right now.

But...what apartment was he talking about? And where had they gone? And why were the idiots out so close to sunrise?

Seemed like we both had a lot to catch up on. I held back my questions for the moment, wanting to ask about a million of them at once. Ethan was right, we needed to get moving. Once night fell on this city, I had no doubt Raphael would be making moves to get me back into his grasp.

And this time my guys might not survive the fight. Even now we weren't safe—not if Amala could open a portal anywhere she pleased. I really had no idea how that worked. We needed to move. And to keep moving.

"Right," I said, bringing myself back to the present. "But I'm not going there like this." I gestured down at my blood-soaked black tank top and leather pants. Nothing I was wearing had been properly washed since Raphael had captured me. I smelled horribly of blood, sweat, and stale washing from the attempts I made to clean my things in the bathroom sink.

If it was between wearing my dirty clothes or go naked like the others, I was going to have to stink. But now the side of my tank and entire left side of my leather pants were chewed up from where I'd scraped along the asphalt after Ethan managed to pluck me out of the air. He must have lost his grip on me, but at least he'd dulled the impact.

Now that I was taking stock, I thought my ribs might be cracked, but it was nothing I hadn't dealt with before. Nothing felt like it had been completely broken. I would deal.

Ethan's soft brown eyes roved over me and then fell on the door leading out into the shopping mall. He nodded. "Alright. I guess I'll need something to cover myself, too." He reached out and brushed a piece of grit from my cheek with the brush of his thumb and then held his hand there for a second, as if checking to make sure what he was seeing was real. He drew in a ragged breath and his lips pulled up in the barest of grin. "But quickly. And we stay together."

I put my hand in his.

"Together."

CHAPTER 23

I could hear them the moment we stepped out of the elevator on the fourteenth floor. Strangely, the metal box didn't faze me as much as it usually did. Ethan, ever the gentleman, had offered to take the stairs with me, but I didn't want to wait another second to see them.

They were arguing. That much was clear. The raised voices coming from the room down the hall could only be my guys. The bellowing roar of Frost, and the responding lethal hiss of Blake.

I couldn't hear Azrael at all and wondered if he was even in there with them.

Ethan gave me an impish grin as we approached the door, an apology in his eyes.

He leaned into my side, "You sure you want to go in there?" he joked.

I smiled back, smoothing out the front of my Black Sabbath t-shirt. Ethan looked adorable in his Zelda one, and I was reminded of how much he liked that game when we were kids. He'd have lived in that world if he could've. His other shirt had been ruined from all the blood on my face, and I was happy to compel him a new one.

I reached out and squeezed his hand. "Let's go shut them up."

Not even a second after I'd spoken, the fighting on the other side of the door stopped and Ethan pushed it open.

The space was wide, with floor to ceiling widows coated in a thick layer of black paint. A pair of huge binoculars lay on a table next to a spot in the window that hadn't been painted, but instead was covered with a flap of newspaper duct taped to the painted glass.

Frost was hovering over Blake like a dark cloud, his face reddened and contorted with rage. Blake held his ground next to the giant, bracing himself for a solid hit from his friend...which looked like it had been about to be thrown just before the door opened.

Now the pair stared in stupefied silence at me and Ethan in the doorway. Frost's expression slackened. His balled right fist lowered.

Blake's dark eyes widened as they took me in toes to tip. He wasn't breathing.

"Rose?"

I shuddered at the sound of his voice and snapped my attention to a desk pressed against the opposite side of the room, strewn with papers and carrying three large monitors. Behind them stood Azrael. His mismatched eyes bored into me and my mind reeled back into the memory.

Dull dead eyes. A gaping wound in my mother's chest where her heart used to be. Blood pooling. Spreading.

A feral cry.

I squinted my eyes shut and looked away, trying to catch my breath. When I opened my eyes again, Azrael was staring at me in horror. And as though my mind *wanted* to share the atrocities I'd had to witness and endure since his twin had taken me from them, my mind vomited it all into my conscious thoughts.

The women and what he was doing with them. What he wanted with me. What he did to me. What he *planned* to do with me still.

I conveyed it all in the blink of an eye, and then I couldn't look at him anymore. Not when all I saw when I met his stony gaze was the memory of his brother. Bile rose in my throat.

Shocking the room into motion, Azrael roared and lifted the heavy metal and leather chair he'd been sitting on against the wall, embedding it there in the drywall and I-beam like some strange sort of artwork.

He shook with barely concealed rage as he stormed past us out of the apartment. It took everything I had not to run like a scared rat away from his approach. I only breathed once he was gone, a pain jabbing into my chest. I didn't want Azrael to hurt. Not because of me. I didn't want to be afraid of his face.

But...I couldn't help it. Not right now. I'd talk to him later. Once I was able to separate who he was from the monster I saw when I looked into his eyes. *He's not his brother.* I knew that now, with more certainty than I ever had before.

Frost and Blake were jolted out of their shock from the loud noise and were practically crawling over one another in their haste to get to me. I met them halfway, stepping over a strange line of what looked like salt and ashes in the doorway. I fell between them as they wrapped their arms around me, effectively making a Rose sandwich.

I couldn't breathe from how tightly they were crushing me, but I didn't care.

"Rosie, baby, you're back," Frost croaked.

"Only our Rose could get herself out of a building filled with over two hundred vampires," I heard Ethan say proudly from somewhere beyond the walls of muscle and flesh barring me in.

Had he said *two-hundred?*

Fuck.

I was glad I didn't know that.

"*And* survive jumping from a sixty-foot-tall building..."

I winced.

"You did *what?*" Frost growled, his hands circling my arms to hold me in place as he searched my face.

Unperturbed for once at his brusque behavior, I just grinned. "I *escaped.* Does it really matter how?" I glanced back at Ethan, who was standing smugly with his hands crossed over his chest and a smirk playing on his lips—radiating pride. "But I had a little help."

I mouthed *thank you* to Ethan and he nodded.

Frost's grip on my arms loosened and Blake tugged me out of Frost's grasp, tucking me into his chest. "*Easy*," he warned Frost, his tone sharp.

Frost's nostrils flared, but he didn't argue.

I nuzzled into Blake, taking a deep breath of clean linen and suede. "I missed you," I said, suddenly aware of how exhausted I was. Now that I was here. Now that I was as safe as I could be right now.

"How did you get out?" Blake asked, still holding me tightly in a rare embrace. Even my tight returning hug didn't seem to bother him much right then. I soaked it up while I could before the moment passed.

I stifled a yawn while trying to reply.

"I think she needs to sleep," Ethan said. "Judging by those circles under her eyes and how pale she is...well, I don't think she's had much. Have you?"

I pursed my lips, but there was no sense in lying. I was sure the whole ordeal was written all over my face. "Not much," I admitted. "But we can't stay here. It was Amala who grabbed me last time. *Through a fucking portal.* If she found me in Phoenix, she'll be able to find me again here. Find *us*."

I really didn't want to go anywhere. I wanted to curl up on the carpet right where I was standing and sleep.

"The line around the apartment," Ethan said with a jerk of his chin toward the door. I noticed the line I'd stepped over to come in again. A thick bar of salt and black ash. Except this time, I noticed how it wasn't just in front of the door, but ran the length of the walls, the entire way around the room. "As long as we're inside it and it remains unbroken, she can't find us."

"What happened in Italy?" I asked, wondering uneasily about Estelle, Valentina, and the others. "Did they come for you there?"

Ethan frowned. "No. We evacuated just to be safe, but with only me and a few of the weaker vamps there, I can't imagine the witch thought we were much of a threat—I mean, since she didn't know what I was doing with your blood."

So, I had been right then...

"Where are they? Where are the vampires?"

Blake adjusted his hold on me and Frost, calmer now, pointed to the bank of monitors atop the desk where Azrael had been when we'd first returned. I wondered where he went but couldn't think about that right now. He just better not be doing anything fucking stupid...like storming a building with two hundred vampires inside of it.

"See for yourself," Frost grunted.

Curious, I went over to the monitors on leaden legs and placed my palms against the desk, leaning in for a better look. There were images on the screens. Six little boxes on each. Within each window was a livestreamed feed. Vampires as far as the eye could see.

Vampires sleeping. Vampires fucking. Vampires sipping from blood bags and chatting. So many vampires. I could tell after a moment that there were three different locations being shown on the feeds. All converted warehouse type spaces like the ones Azrael owned.

After a few more seconds, I was able to identify the first group of vamps we'd brought on board from Naples. And then, after a few seconds more, I found Valentina, looking radiant and alight with life. She was surrounded by three males and I smirked. She was accepting her new role in the immortal world even better than I'd hoped. I was sure it helped that they were all fantastically gorgeous.

My brows knit together as my tired mind tried to percolate what this meant. "How many are there?"

"Over one-fifty," Blake said with a mischievous grin.

"How in the hell did you—"

"Losing you was probably the best possible motivator," Ethan interrupted, explaining. "We've been taking shifts watching the building and going out to gather vampires to our cause."

"It was the best compromise," Blake added.

I cocked my head at him, trying to catch on.

"We wanted to go in and get you," Frost said, his tone telling me he was still pissed, but trying hard to get control. "But fuckface wouldn't let us. He said we would all die, and you would blame him."

I scoffed, pushing off from the desk to find myself woozy from the sudden motion. "Well, he was right. When I was in there, I *prayed* you guys wouldn't be stupid enough to try to break me out."

"The question is, how did *you* manage to get out?"

I sighed, my shoulders sagging as deep exhaustion settled into my bones, making gravity seem stronger than it had only a few moments before.

Ethan's hands came to rest on my shoulders, lending me some of his strength. "She'll explain everything when she's ready," Ethan said, squeezing my shoulders gently. "Won't you?"

I nodded numbly, my gaze flitting up from the clusters of vampires on the monitors to find there was a lab, much like the one Ethan had set up in Azrael's mansion, except this one taking over a large stainless steel kitchen in the corner.

I groaned. Looking between the screens and Ethan's new lab. "How long have they been waiting?" I mumbled, sagging back into Ethan, barely able to hold my own weight anymore.

"What did she say?" Frost barked, leaning in.

I hadn't realized how low my voice had gotten as a heaviness settled over my chest. I started to wonder if I'd hemorrhaged something while trying to break Rafe's compulsion. I had bled *a lot*.

Ethan's arm wrapped around my back and he bent to latch his other beneath my knees, lifting me to his chest. I leaned my head against his breast, eyes burning from trying to stay conscious. His nautical scent wrapped around me like a summer's breeze, and I was brought back to a simpler time.

A time when the four of us sat together on the beach, sand in our shorts and between our toes. The warm sun brushing against our cheeks as the cool evening breeze tugged our hair. All of us huddled beneath that ratty old blanket with the mathematical equations on it that Ethan always brought with us. Borrowing warmth from each other. Finding comfort in one another's touch.

I wanted that back. I sank into the memory, wishing we all could've stayed there in the sand.

"She asked how long they've been waiting," he repeated to Frost, a bite in his voice. "They were all promised a taste of the sun in return for their allegiance," he trailed off, letting his words sink in.

There was a crashing sound and I flinched, still trying to fight the claws of darkness trying to claim me. Slipping into and out of the memory of simpler times with my guys.

"Don't fight," I tried to tell them, but the words came out a barely audible mumble.

Someone brushed the hair out of my face, and I smelled the scent of clean linen as Blake leaned in to plant a kiss on my forehead. His voice was hard as steel as he said, "She's going to need to bleed."

I felt more than saw Ethan nod his agreement. "Yes," he said solemnly. "She is."

"When will this end?" Frost's gritty bellow boomed through the room and ricocheted in my skull. I whimpered into Ethan's chest, wishing I had the strength left to cover my ears. I didn't want to hear them argue. Not now.

"It will end when he's *dead*," Azrael's voice had my eyes snapping open and a hiss tearing from my throat.

"Please," I mumbled as discordant thoughts and images crowded my mind. "No."

"She needs to rest. She almost killed herself to break

my brother's compulsion. She needs to heal." Azrael's voice was distant. Detached.

I shook in Ethan's arms.

"What is it, Rose?"

I clutched at his t-shirt and buried my face in his scent. "Get me away from him," I managed. "I can't..."

"Can't what?"

"Not yet..."

Ethan turned away and carried me into a dark space, setting me down on a mattress that smelled distinctly of all of my guys. Their mingled scents brought me the comfort I needed to relax my burning muscles. He moved to pull away, but I caught his hand.

"Don't leave," I murmured, sinking beneath a blanket that felt softer than a cloud.

Ethan's weight pressed into the mattress next to me and I inched closer to him until I was securely in his embrace, warm and more comfortable than I could remember being in much too long.

"I won't," he said in a whisper, and I felt the press of his chin on top of my head. "I'll be here as long as you need, my queen."

Before I could fully drift off, I melted into him, pressing my lips to his collarbone. I tried to speak again, but it was like my lips and tongue were no longer properly connected. "I...love..."

Ethan hushed me. "*Sleep*," he ordered. "Tell me when you wake."

Continue Rose's story in DESTROY ME, The Last Vocari, Book 4!